Highroller's Man

Center Point
Large Print

Also by Ray Hogan and available from Center Point Large Print:

Jackman's Wolf
The Yesterday Rider
The Iron Jehu
The Doomsday Trail
The Outlawed
The Crosshatch Men
Pilgrim
The Renegade Gun
Betrayal in Tombstone

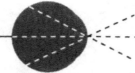

This Large Print Book carries the Seal of Approval of N.A.V.H.

Highroller's Man

A Shawn Starbuck Western

RAY HOGAN

CENTER POINT LARGE PRINT
THORNDIKE, MAINE

This Center Point Large Print edition
is published in the year 2024 by arrangement with
Golden West Inc.

Copyright © 1973 by Ray Hogan.
Copyright © renewed 2001 by Gwynn Henline.

All rights reserved.

Originally published in the US by Signet.

The text of this Large Print edition is unabridged.
In other aspects, this book may vary
from the original edition.
Printed in the United States of America
on permanent paper sourced using
environmentally responsible foresting methods.
Set in 16-point Times New Roman type.

ISBN 979-8-89164-007-8 (hardcover)
ISBN 979-8-89164-011-5 (paperback)

The Library of Congress has cataloged this record
under Library of Congress Control Number: 2023946257

1

It was sunlight glinting off the worn surface of a rifle barrel that warned Shawn Starbuck. A tall, muscular man with dark hair and gray-blue eyes, he stood quietly, body tensed, at the edge of the crowd gathering to hear Orville Flood make his speech, and probed the source of the flash with exacting care.

The brief flicker had come from the roof of a hardware store on the opposite side of the square that was the town of San Ignacio's public meeting place. He could see no one, but a man had been there, one with but a single purpose in mind—kill Orville Flood.

Shawn continued to study the building, carefully searching every foot of its false-fronted roof with his gaze. Although Flood was a person he scarcely knew, the man's safety was important to him; the five hundred in gold that Orville's brother Carl and other members of the Central Party committee in Santa Fe had agreed to pay him for his services as bodyguard was contingent on his getting their candidate through the campaign alive.

If anything happened to Flood on his swing through the Territory, there would be no pay; that was the agreement. He'd had his choice at the start—a hundred a month for the estimated sixty-day period the campaign would cover, regardless of what occurred, or five hundred for the same length of time, but payable only if Orville completed the tour unscathed. It had been an easy decision for Starbuck to make.

Five hundred dollars represented sufficient capital to keep him on the move for many months in his search for his brother Ben. It wouldn't be necessary, as it had in the past, to halt, find a job, and rebuild his finances; and, too, he was confident enough of his own abilities to risk all or nothing on such an offer—this despite Flood's daughter, Carla, and the fact that the Central Party committee had been warned their candidate faced assassination if he pursued his course of opposition to statehood and continued to espouse the sale of a vast, lush region known as the *Pastizal* to a foreign syndicate that had plans for entering the cattle-raising business.

The opposing Statehood Party denied, of course, all connection with anyone promising murder, and insisted it was no part of their program in their effort to elect Tom Josson, who stood for statehood and the opening of the *Pastizal* to homesteaders and other settlers.

They advanced the theory that the threat came from someone entirely outside the political arena—a disgruntled land owner, perhaps, or a rancher fearing the strong competition a large, moneyed beef-growing syndicate would present; or possibly it was some fanatically loyal resident who believed not only in statehood but in the retention of the *Pastizal* for the use of the general public as well.

The Central Party had expected the denial, of course, and greeted it with knowing smiles and suitable remarks to the newspapers. But they were not fools, and had turned to the U.S. marshal for aid. He advised them that his office could in no way afford continuing protection, and suggested they hire an able bodyguard to do the job. Asked to suggest such a person, he referred them to Starbuck, with whom he'd had similar dealings in the past.

Shawn, riding out the winter months in Tucson after failing to overtake Ben in either Wickenburg or the old mission city, was on the verge of moving on west when the letter came. He was not surprised to hear from the marshal; it was his practice to let the various lawmen with whom he'd become acquainted around the country know of his whereabouts on the chance they would encounter Ben or get word concerning him. He was surprised, however, at the offer that was being made to him, and loading his gear, he mounted his sorrel gelding and made the trip to Santa Fe in near record time.

One slight drawback had developed, however. When the proposition had been laid before him at the beginning it involved only Orville Flood and his protection. Two weeks later when he met Flood and the chartered stagecoach in which the man planned to visit all of the important towns in the Territory, Flood had rung in his daughter Carla.

A pert, blue-eyed, exquisitely assembled twenty-year-old, she was just out of an Eastern finishing school. In addition to her undeniable beauty, Carla was also endowed with a self-proclaimed depth of wisdom that freshly turned graduates of schools of higher learning sometimes seem to feel they alone possess; she had a supercilious attitude toward the West and the people who populated its broad reaches, and a tongue sharp as the proverbial serpent's tooth.

She and Shawn had clashed shortly after meeting, and had he not given his word to stay on the job regardless of all else, it is likely he would have chucked the whole affair, reinstated his original plans to head west, and ridden on. But he stuck to his bargain, and now, with the journey well under way, a sort of uneasy truce lay between them, one interrupted occasionally by outbursts of bitter words on the part of Carla, who felt Starbuck's shepherding was more of a hindrance to her father than a help. . . .

As he worked his way along the edge of the gathering, Shawn glanced over his shoulder. Flood, followed by his daughter, had emerged from the hotel and was walking slowly toward the raised platform in the center of the plaza from which he would do his speaking. His progress was gradual, for he was being halted every few steps by well-wishers.

Starbuck gained a position at the rear of the square, where he had an unrestricted view, and again shifted his eyes to the rooftop of the hardware store where he had seen the flash of metal. The sounds of the crowd—shouts, laughter, loud talking, the crying of a child, the steady thump of a bass drum—now filled the dust-charged warm air, but he gave no thought to such; his attention was wholly claimed by the possibility of danger to Orville Flood.

There was still no sign of life on the top of the building, and he pushed on, shouldering his way through the thickening crowd, following a parallel course that would afford him a continuous view of the structure. Farther on he could see Frank Ogden, the coach driver hired by the committee, squatting in the shade at the side of the livery stable. He could use the old driver's help, Shawn thought, but Ogden, head tipped forward, was apparently dozing.

On beyond him, on the steps of a saloon, Starbuck caught a glimpse of Pete Ditzler, the local town marshal, and realized he could expect no help from him either. Earlier he'd spoken to the man about the need for extra deputies during

Flood's speech, but the lawman had waved aside the request. Hell, he knew every man, woman, and child in the goddammed county—and none of them'd be taking potshots at Orville Flood, no sir!

"Not doubting that," Shawn had said, hanging tight to his temper. "It's the outsiders that worry me."

Ditzler, flanked by several friends, had turned stiff and resentful after that. He'd hooked his thumbs in his gunbelt and said, "Now, maybe you are the handy-andy them big wheels in Santa Fe hired on to wet-nurse their boy, but that don't mean nothing around here! In my town it's me that keeps the peace—not some trigger-happy gunny who—"

"Let it drop there," Starbuck had drawled softly, stilling the marshal's rash words. "Way I understand it, you won't give me any help."

"Nope, because you plain won't be needing none. I know this place."

Shawn had moved off, no stranger to Pete Ditzler's attitude, which he'd encountered previously in other settlements. Now, however, thinking it over, he wished he'd ignored Ditzler's enmity and his own irritation, and had insisted that deputies be scattered about the square; folks didn't realize how tense the issue between the two political factions had become—particularly over the question of the *Pastizal*.

He came to a halt, gazed again at the store's roof. What he could see looked innocent enough, but now, due to his nearness, a part of the building was blocking his view. He'd be better off at a distance. Dissatisfied, he began to work his way back across the square toward the speaker's platform. Orville and Carla had ascended the stand. The girl had taken a chair at the rear, alongside several of San Ignacio's more important citizens. She flicked him with a cool glance as he mounted the steps and moved in behind Flood, who stood posed in the center of the platform, arms raised as he called for silence.

Carla, as usual, appeared bored. It was always thus, and he wondered again why she had chosen to come and be with her father. She did not fit; her remote manner, her stylish dress, her precise way of speaking, were in direct contrast to the rough-and-ready, down-to-earth sort of folks who made up the gatherings they solicited, and she forever, intentionally or not, gave the impression of placing herself above all she encountered.

But if her manner was of no help to Flood, Starbuck had to concede that she evened things up by helping her father with his speeches, by seeing to it that he ate and rested properly, and by simply being with him where her beauty was a natural attraction.

"Good friends . . ."

Shawn's eyes swept over the crowd and then

settled once more on the roof of the hardware store as Flood began his oration. Almost at once he saw a dull flash of light. An instant later a blurred face, all but hidden by a stained, ragged hat, appeared—and then the flicker of light on metal as a rifle barrel was leveled at the man in the center of the platform.

"Look out!" Starbuck shouted.

2

Starbuck triggered a shot at the bushwhacker on the roof and lunged at Flood. His shoulder caught the man from behind and knocked him sprawling to the dusty floor. Startled yells went up from the suddenly confused and milling crowd, and he heard Carla cry out at him in an angry voice, but he ignored her.

Regaining his balance, he leaped from the stand and began to bull his way through the press of people rushing to clear the area around the speaker's platform. Midway across the plaza he threw a second bullet at the roof's false front, aiming at the point where he had seen the sniper and hopeful of keeping him pinned down until he could close in and effect a capture.

More shouts lifted at the report, and the crowd, quickly giving way before his grim-faced approach, now shifted and began to flow toward the street. From the tail of his eye Shawn could see Frank Ogden running toward him. Raising a hand, Starbuck motioned at the hardware store. Whether or not the driver saw him, he could not tell.

Reaching the building, he faced down the narrow, weed-choked passageway that lay between it and the adjacent structure. A thin, gray mist of dust hung in the air, and from beyond the row of houses farther on came the drumming tattoo of a fast-running horse.

Starbuck swore. He was too late. The sniper had evidently picketed his horse at the back of the store, just under the eaves of the low, slanted roof. It had been easy for him to drop onto the saddle and make an escape. Shawn cursed again. If that damn Ditzler had given him some deputies, let him spot them around, he just might have been able to put an end to at least one threat that was hanging over Orville Flood's head!

Seething, Starbuck pivoted, retraced his steps to the square. The gathering had scattered, and only a few people were in evidence now, standing about in small groups talking among themselves. Flood, face flushed with anger, sided by an equally infuriated Carla, glared down at him from the deserted platform. But it was Ditzler, bustling across the plaza, features working with indignation, who stopped him.

"What the devil's the matter with you?" he demanded at a shout. "Ain't you got no better sense'n to go emptying your gun in a crowd like this? Could've got some folks tromped to—"

"Was a man up there with a rifle," Shawn cut in coolly. "Had a bead on Flood."

Disbelief filled the lawman's eyes. "A killer hiding up there—you sure?"

"I'm sure," Starbuck snapped, and started up

the steps to the platform. Behind him he heard Ditzler voice a question to what remained of the gathering.

"Any of you see somebody up on Girard's roof? This here highroller's man says there was."

There was a murmur of negative replies. Shawn shrugged. Such was to be expected; anyone facing Orville Flood would have his back to the hardware store and could not have noticed the bushwhacker. Gaining the stand, he focused his attention on Flood. The man had a small scratch on his cheek, and dust marked the front of his dark suit from the fall he had taken. His eyes were sparking.

"See here, Starbuck—I've taken all the interference—"

"Interference!" Shawn cut in impatiently. He brushed at the sweat on his forehead. "If I hadn't knocked you flat you'd be a dead man right now!"

"I doubt that," Carla said icily. "I think it was just another of your tricks!"

Starbuck's jaw hardened as he fought to control his temper. After a moment he managed a faint, humorless smile, the end result of an upbringing by Clare and Hiram Starbuck, who had taught him that women, regardless of the situation, are owed respect and consideration.

"Hardly a trick," he said quietly.

"I think it was—just as I think those other incidents we've endured were tricks—interruptions designed to interfere with my father's work. I'm beginning to wonder if you aren't working for the other side."

"You're right to think what you please." Shawn swung his attention to Orville Flood. "You got the same idea?"

"It does begin to appear that way," the man said, frowning. "It seems that just about every time I get a good crowd together for a meeting, you find some excuse to break it up."

"After today, I don't think we need any further proof that you are against us," Carla added in her prim, definite way.

"Like I said, think what you please. Fact is, I don't give a damn one way or another who wins or loses in this election. I'm only interested in getting paid for the job I signed on for—keeping your pa alive—"

"Say, you, highroller's man!"

Shawn turned to the square again at the sound of Ditzler's voice, vaguely irritated by the term being applied to him, even though it was in common usage where the political group officially known as the Central Party committee was concerned.

"Yeah?"

"Done some asking around. Ain't nobody seen a man up on Girard's roof—not today or any other day. You dang sure you ain't had maybe a couple of shots of redeye too many?"

The men gathered around Pete Ditzler laughed, then sobered as Starbuck touched them with a cold glance. "He was there."

The lawman wagged his head. "Then what d'you reckon happened to him?"

"Time I got to the back of that store, he was gone. Reason I wanted some deputies—"

"You see what kind of a horse he was riding?" Ditzler broke in hastily.

"Too late for that. He was already on the yonder side of the houses back there. All I can tell you is he was wearing an old, dark hat, plenty dirty and with the brim chewed up, and he was carrying a rifle."

There was a moment's silence during which Ditzler rubbed at his jaw, then, "Well, all I can say is that it's dang funny nobody else seen him."

"No one else could have," Carla Flood commented pointedly, and faced her father. "I think the time has come for you to do something about it."

Orville nodded briskly. "Starbuck, like for you to understand this—"

Shawn drew himself up stiffly, folded his arms across his chest. Off down the street the sound of hammering could be heard as if a carpenter, having interrupted his work that he might listen to Flood, had now resumed his labors.

"Winning this election is important not only to the men who are backing me but to my daughter and me as well." Orville Flood's voice was high, intense. "Fact is, we've staked everything on it and I cannot permit anything to hinder my chances."

Shawn remained silent, nodding his understanding.

"Therefore, there's only one thing left for me to do—ask you to resign your job—quit."

Starbuck's long lips pulled into a tight smile. "No, not about to do that. Expect to do the job I was hired for."

"I can refuse to let you stay around—"

"You could try, but it wouldn't do any good. I'd still be somewhere close. . . . One thing you'd best get straight, it wasn't you that hired me or that'll be paying me when it's finished."

"Perhaps, but I can send a telegram to them—to my brother—demand they fire you!"

"Go ahead. Not sure they'll pay much heed. Meetings of yours that I've busted up or put a crimp into were ones where you might've gotten bad hurt or killed—like today. Been others where you got to do your talking—"

"Small gatherings that weren't of much help!" Carla said scornfully. "The large ones, you always manage to spoil."

"For the simple reason they're the ones where trouble has shown up," Shawn replied, beginning to grow weary of the incessant arguing. "Maybe you didn't see that man on the roof today but there's been times before this when you saw—"

"We saw things—men—that you *claimed* could be dangerous," the girl cut in. "I'm not sure, after what's happened today, that there was any danger."

Starbuck shrugged. "No, I was just having me some fun," he said, and turned toward the steps.

"I still plan to send that telegram—as soon as we get to a town where there's an office," Flood called after him.

"Suit yourself. Meantime, I'll hang around—"

"You won't be welcome!" Carla said waspishly.

He paused, then grinned at her. "Have I ever been?" he asked, and continued on.

3

Two hours later they were again on the road. Flood had salvaged the stopover in San Ignacio to some extent by making a brief speech to a small crowd at the edge of town, after which they pushed on for Bonnerville, one of the larger and more important settlements on the itinerary. With luck they would reach it by dark, which was what the schedule called for since Flood was to meet in debate with his principal opponent, Tom Josson, the following day.

Ordinarily Starbuck preferred to be in the saddle during the passage from town to town. Such permitted him to range ahead and keep a close watch on the country for signs of trouble. But this time, turned morose by his exchange of words with the Floods, disturbed by the first real attempt on the man's life, and worried about the coming day when the killer would likely try again, he had altered his usual pattern by tying his sorrel gelding to the rear of the coach and taking a seat beside the driver.

Frank Ogden—a spare, wintery oldster with faded eyes and a stringy mustache—braced himself on the box with one foot against the brake, and lacing the lines of the four-horse team between the fingers of his left hand, considered Shawn speculatively.

"You're so quiet I can hear you sweating," he drawled. "What's bothering you most—losing that killer or maybe losing your job?"

Starbuck leaned back in the seat. "Letting him get away. Means trouble tomorrow. You see him?"

"Nope, but you saying you did's enough for me."

"Obliged to you for that. Don't much appreciate being called a liar by a whole town."

"Reckon we can blame that two-bit marshal for him still running loose. If he'd done what you asked—"

Starbuck shrugged, his glance sweeping the distant smudged edges of the flat across which they were rushing. There was little point in hashing over what was past; his chance to apprehend the would-be killer had escaped him, and the situation would have to be faced again.

Ogden shifted the lines to his other hand and shouted at the team as they dipped into an arroyo, then pounded up the opposite side. "Who you reckon it is that's got it in for Orville?" he asked.

"Can't even guess—and I don't figure it's so much him they're after as it is what he stands for and what he wants to do. This *Pastizal*, that's the big rub. Lots of folks are against selling it to some big syndicate. They want to see it opened up for ranching and homesteading."

Ogden bobbed his head, spat into the spinning spokes of the wheel below him. "Yeah, old Orville sure plowed up a lot of snakes there. . . . Losing this here job, you going to mind it much?"

"Haven't lost it yet, but if I do I expect I'll go right on living. Thing that bothers me most isn't that, it's Flood himself—and his daughter. Just can't make them believe he's liable to get killed, and whether I lose the job or not's unimportant when it comes to a man's life."

"Them two are a caution, all right. And that little gal, she's just about as friendly as a grizzly bear with the frostbite."

Starbuck smiled, as he nodded. The coach whirled on over the rutted road, rocking and creaking on its leather springs, dropping into the shallow washes, rushing up the far sides as the horses churned the dry earth beneath their hooves into a fine, gray powder. Overhead the sky was cloudless, a vast ocean of blue from which the unobscured sun bore down relentlessly.

"Reckon if you do lose out you'll pick up where you left off and start hunting that brother you was telling me about."

At the driver's words, Shawn stirred, looking for a more comfortable position on the seat. "Have to find myself a job first. Wasn't much work around Tucson. Poke's got a bit flat."

"Jobs ain't so plentiful nowhere. . . . You never

did say why this here brother left home and why you're needing to find him—or ain't it any of my business?"

"I don't mind telling you. My folks had a farm back in Ohio, on the Muskingum River. Ben and I were born there. Pa was a good man but a mite strict. He and Ben got into it one day over some chores Ben forgot to do. Ended up with Ben leaving, saying he'd never come back—that he was even going to change his name."

Ogden shifted the pumping leathers from his left to his right hand, easing his shoulder. "Did he?"

"Yeah. Goes by the name of Damon Friend now. Was some time before I found that out."

"You ain't never ever got close enough to even talk to him?"

"Never that close. Almost caught up a few times, but not quite."

"It real important you catch him?"

"Pa left a pretty fair amount of money in his estate. Can't be touched until I find Ben, take him back home to meet the lawyer handling things. Then it'll be divided between us two."

"What if he's dead?"

"Isn't—at least he wasn't last October. Traced him to Wickenburg—over in Arizona—then down to Tucson. Lost him there. If things don't work out for me on this job, I'll head back that way, maybe go on into Mexico soon as I've raised some cash. Sort of got a hunch he crossed the border."

"But what if he does turn up dead? You lose your part of the money?"

"No, just have to furnish proof that he is dead—"

"Rider coming," Ogden said laconically.

Shawn had caught sight of the man at the same moment—a lone figure moving out of a grove of cottonwoods to their right, and angling toward the road. As the gap between them narrowed, the horseman raised a staying hand.

"You want me to stop?" the old driver asked.

Starbuck continued to study the approaching rider, slouched to one side on his saddle as he jogged up at a lazy pace. He was wearing a large black hat, Shawn noted, and the tension within him lessened considerably.

"Go ahead, pull in," he said.

"He's a Mex," Ogden commented, bringing the coach to a halt. "Must be some kind of trouble somewheres."

Starbuck got to his feet, left hand hanging loosely above the pistol he wore. Half turning, he directed his voice to the inside of the vehicle.

"You folks stay put," he said, and swung his attention back to the vaquero.

"Could get yourself shot, trying that."

The Mexican kneed his horse in nearer. He was a dark, slim man with black, restless eyes.

"I am sorry, senor. A little water, *por favor.*"

Ogden tossed the canteen to him. "This ain't no place to get caught without water, for sure."

The vaquero nodded gravely, smiled, and pulling the cork from the container, raised the canteen to his lips. He paused, a frown knitting his brow. "It is strange to see a stagecoach here. It is one of a special nature, perhaps?"

"Just taking a shortcut to—" Starbuck began, but he broke off as the door of the vehicle opened and Flood stepped out. "Damn him," he finished angrily at low breath.

"Name's Orville Flood," the man said, moving to the Mexican, hand extended. "Could be you've heard of me."

The vaquero lowered the canteen, took Flood's fingers into his own. "Cruz Mendoza, senor, at your service," he murmured politely. "*Si*, in truth I have heard much of you."

"Good things, I hope," Flood said heartily. He was a middle-aged man, a bit on the squat side, with friendly eyes and a wide, engaging smile.

Mendoza continued to grin. "Such is so—a very fine man, I am told."

Flood beamed. "I trust that means you and your friends will support me in the coming election," he said, looking expectantly over his shoulder toward the coach. "My daughter—"

Carla appeared, poised on the edge of the seat, with one slippered foot resting daintily on the sill of the open door. In the afternoon sunshine the red highlights in her dark hair shone brightly.

"—My daughter, Mr. Mendoza."

The vaquero swept off his broad-brimmed hat and bowed slightly. "It is my pleasure, senorita."

Carla gave him her fixed smile. "I am happy to meet you, Mr. Mendoza. I hope my father can count on you and your friends—"

"It is a certainty, senorita."

Flood slapped his palms together, rubbing them briskly. "Why don't you come to Bonnerville tomorrow," he suggested. "I'll be making a speech there—in fact, my opponent will be on hand, too. We plan to debate the issues. I'm sure you'll find it interesting."

"Such would be a pleasure, senor Flood."

"There are many things that need to be brought to the attention of the Spanish and Mexican people, one of which—"

"Time we moved on," Starbuck broke in firmly. "Got to make Bonnerville by dark."

Carla's lips tightened as she touched him with a withering glance, and then pulled herself back into the coach. Orville Flood frowned, displaying his annoyance, but he nodded to the vaquero and smiled, trying to mask his displeasure.

"Expect we had best be on our way," he said, offering his hand. "I'll look forward to seeing you and some of your friends tomorrow."

"You do us a great honor, senor," Mendoza

26

replied, accepting the farewell gesture. "*Adios.*"

Flood pivoted, crawled stiffly back into the coach, and slammed the door. The vaquero, still smiling, edged in nearer to Ogden and returned the canteen to him.

"*Muchas gracias,*" he said in his soft, sibilant tongue. "We shall meet again, eh?"

"Could be," the old driver answered, and slapping the reins against the backs of his team, sent the coach lurching forward.

Starbuck, again seated beside Ogden, kept his eyes on the Mexican, as yet unmoving on the road. After a time he turned back, the flat planes of his face set and thoughtful. The driver spat into the wheel.

"Well, expect you stuck another burr under old Orville's blanket, rushing him off the way you done. He was just about to tell that Mex how they all've been—"

"Yeah, I've heard it, too," Starbuck murmured.

Ogden looked at him more closely. "Something's ragging you. Was it Mendoza?"

Shawn nodded.

"What about him? Seems a likable sort of fellow."

"Just this. Stopped us claiming he needed water, but he never did get around to taking a drink. Way that adds up for me is he came for some other reason."

4

They whirled into Bonnerville shortly before sundown. A much larger settlement than Shawn expected, it lay in a broad bowl of land beyond which a ragged, towering mass of mountains formed a smoky backdrop.

There appeared to be one main street, with three or four lesser avenues intersecting and an equal number paralleling. Twin rows of high, false-fronted buildings stood along the primary thoroughfare, facing each other through a sunlit wall of drifting, tan dust. The town was crowded. People were milling about and there was a gay, carnival-like atmosphere, evidence of the interest being taken in the coming debate between Flood and Tom Josson.

In a park somewhere near the center of the settlement the familiar speaker's platform had been erected. Red, white, and blue bunting draped the rough pine boards that had been used in its construction. A canopy of canvas had been stretched overhead to protect the dignitaries from the sun. Shawn viewed it with satisfaction as they passed; it would also shield those on the stand from the eyes of any sniper who might be hiding on the roof of a nearby business. Such would be of great help; there was little doubt the crowd that would be in attendance was going to be large.

"Reckon you got your work cut out for you," Ogden said as he drove slowly down the street in search of the hotel. "Looks like about half the Territory's here."

Starbuck nodded his agreement. Faces were turned toward them, smiling, curious. He let his glance rake all those along the way; he too was searching, but for a man with a torn brimmed hat or anyone else who showed signs of hostility.

"There she is," Ogden said abruptly, and immediately cut sharp right.

They stopped before a two-storied building above the door of which a freshly painted sign proclaimed THE WESTERN STAR HOTEL. Instantly people in the near vicinity gravitated toward the coach, suspecting that it conveyed one or the other of the two celebrities.

Starbuck rose hurriedly, scrutinized the gathering with troubled eyes. The experience in San Ignacio, together with the incidents, even if minor, prior to that, and the puzzle of Cruz Mendoza were weighing heavily on his mind. There were too many people, too tightly packed. It would be easy for a man to hide among them, get off a shot from a pistol without being noticed.

He heard Frank Ogden climb down, grunt when his heels struck the ground, and announce superfluously, "Reckon we're here, Mr. Flood."

The coach door squealed drily on its hinges as it opened. Shawn felt the vehicle tip slightly as Flood and Carla stepped out. He caught a glimpse of the girl as she flung a still angry look at him, but instead of turning he continued to watch the growing crowd now pressing in tighter about the stage.

Cheers interlaced with a scattering of catcalls welled up as Flood raised his hands and made some sort of gesture. He was standing in the open, smiling broadly.

"Get inside the hotel—quick," Starbuck snapped. "This bunch could get out of hand."

Flood sobered, frowned. Carla turned and flung Shawn an angry look. "There's no need—" she began.

"Inside—dammit!" he barked.

Flood lowered his head, accepting the order, and with girl preceding him by a step, entered the building. The crowd began to shout and hoot its disapproval. Starbuck ignored the racket, dropped to the board sidewalk.

"What's the matter with him? He afraid to answer some questions?" a tall, spare man in a gray suit demanded.

"Later," Shawn replied, studying the speaker narrowly. "He's had a long day. There something special you want to ask him?"

"Plenty we're all wanting to know about—this

Pastizal for one thing—and why he don't want us becoming a state for another."

Starbuck shrugged. He was overly suspicious, he supposed. "You'll get your chance to talk to him," he said.

"The congressman wants his bags—" The hotel clerk—a small, wizened individual in a shiny blue serge suit and polished yellow, button shoes, donned no doubt for the occasion—bustled up to Ogden.

From the crowd a voice said, "Hell, he ain't elected yet." A burst of laughter went up.

The driver pointed to the rear of the coach. "There, in the boot, just help yourself. Only don't be taking them two little ones. They belong to me and my friend here."

The clerk hurried off on his errand. Ogden moved up to Shawn, still maintaining a close watch over the gradually dispersing group.

"You see anybody familiar?"

Starbuck shook his head. "Be a little hard to recognize anybody that'll mean trouble. Mendoza's the only one I've gotten a good look at."

"And maybe he's all right. We staying here at this hotel?"

Shawn said, "Yes, got us a room close to the Floods."

The driver handed him his bag, took a grip on the handle of his own. "Reckon it's needful, all right. Way it sounded, it ain't everybody that's a friend of Orville's around here."

They entered the lobby of the Western Star, a small square filled with leather chairs and dull-eyed deer heads hanging on the walls. The clerk, now behind his desk, greeted them smilingly.

"Welcome, gents! You must be Mr. Starbuck and Mr. Ogden."

"Your guesser's working good," the old driver said drily.

"Got you fixed up just like your letter wanted. Your room's right across the hall from Mr. Flood and his daughter. Yours is Number Eight. They got Seven and Nine."

Starbuck was only half listening, his attention at the moment drifting about the lobby, resting briefly on each of the two dozen or so men standing about in conversation. There was no sign of the Floods. They apparently had gone directly to their quarters.

"Now, if you'll just register—"

Shawn took the pencil being pushed at him, wrote his name on the soiled page of the book, then passed it to Frank Ogden.

"Full up?" he asked the clerk.

"Yes, sir. Wouldn't have had no room for you if you hadn't wrote ahead for it."

"You wouldn't be full up if we hadn't been coming," Ogden pointed out caustically.

The clerk looked startled, then nodded. "Well,

yes, I reckon that's right. Now, if you're wanting anything just let me know. I'm Ernie Quinn. You just holler if—"

"You noticing a lot of strangers?" Starbuck wondered, again sweeping the room with his glance.

Quinn bobbed happily. "You bet I am! There's a plenty around who ain't never been in town before. It sure is a great day for Bonnerville!"

It was to be expected. The meeting of the two leading political candidates and an airing of their differences had been well publicized. Undoubtedly it was drawing listeners from a considerable distance—which was fine and, after all, the purpose of such an occasion, Shawn realized. And while the majority of those attending would be sincere and interested only in the selection of the better candidate, there would be at least one, possibly even more, with another purpose in mind.

But that was his job, what he'd been hired to guard against—those who would put a bullet into Orville Flood and in that way end his political ambitions. He turned again to Quinn.

"There a restaurant in this building?"

The clerk shook his head. "Nope, take your meals next door—or down the street. We don't get in the eating business and the café people don't rent out beds."

Shawn picked up the key placed on the counter

before him, and followed by Ogden, mounted the stairs. At the top they entered a narrow, shadowy hallway off which numerous doors led, and halted before the one bearing a crudely printed eight. The panel was not locked and they entered, flinching a little as they were met by a blast of stale, hot air. Crossing to the single window, Starbuck threw up the sash. The blank wall of an adjoining building was little more than an arm's length away.

"Sure a mighty fine view," Ogden drawled, tossing his bag onto a chair. He stretched, yawned. "Reckon I'd best see to them horses."

"Go ahead. Aim to clean up a bit. I'll meet you in that restaurant the clerk said was next door in thirty minutes."

"We ain't eating with the Floods?"

Starbuck smiled wryly. "Doubt if they'd welcome my company, but don't let me stop you."

"Reckon I'll stick with you," the old driver said, turning for the door. "That little gal don't exactly admire the way I stow my grub."

Ogden struck off down the hallway, and Shawn, closing the panel and locking it, began to strip. There was water in the china pitcher, and slopping a quantity into its companion bowl, he washed off, shaved, and then drew on a clean shirt. Dressed, he left the room and halted at the door opposite. At his knock Carla Flood's voice answered.

"Who is it?"

"Starbuck."

There was a short delay, and then, clad in a light, quilted robe, she stood before him, serene and cool-looking. "Yes?"

"Everything all right?"

Anger plucked at the corners of her lips and a bright sparkle came into her eyes. "Why, yes, everything is fine!" she said with fine sarcasm. "You spoiled another chance for my father to make friends, you insulted a man who could cause a lot of his people to vote for him—and you ask if everything is all right!"

Starbuck stood silent and motionless, a worn smile his only reaction to her outburst.

From the doorway of the connecting room Orville Flood called, "Who is it, Carla?"

"Mr. Starbuck," she replied. "He wants to know if we're all right."

"Tell him we'll look after ourselves. He doesn't need to bother with us any longer."

"You heard?" Carla asked sweetly.

"I heard—and it means nothing. Restaurant's next door. I'll be waiting there."

"We'll take our meals where and when we please," the girl said stiffly.

"You'll eat next door. I won't have your pa out on the street after dark—and if you're not there in thirty minutes, you'll do without. That clear?"

Starbuck's voice had risen as temper began to

build within him. He started to wheel away, then halted as a sudden gust of frustration and the realization of the futility of trying to reason with the girl or with her father swept through him. Five hundred dollars was a lot of money—sure—and he could use it, but the requirements for earning it were too stiff, too exasperating. He could find another job somewhere that would enable him to raise a little cash so he could continue the search for Ben.

"One thing more," he said with a bitter smile. "There's a telegraph office in this town. Tell your pa to use it. I'm through."

5

Shawn, anger still pounding through him, descended the stairs, stalked through the lobby of the Western Star, and came out onto the porch. He paused there, moved to one side, and leaned against the forward wall of the building. The day's heat had dwindled with the setting sun and a pleasant coolness was closing in, bringing with it a sort of quiet.

But there was no peace within him as he looked out over the people still milling aimlessly about in the street and along the walks fronting the stores. He felt strangely disturbed and at loose ends. Never before had he walked out on a job, and while there had been moments at other times and under similar conditions when he had considered it, he had always brushed aside the desire. It had always seemed to him that it was something closely akin to breaking his word, faulting a trust. But this was different.

He stood there considering the problem while the rancor within him began to ebb slowly. Maybe he had been too hasty. True, he had every reason to chuck the deal, to let Orville Flood and Carla look out for themselves. They simply refused to believe there was any danger involved in the venture they had undertaken; even Flood's brother and the other men backing Orville apparently had failed to convince them.

All right—let them find out for themselves. Let Orville stand up on his speaker's platform and make of himself a target for whoever it was out to kill him. Let him move about through the crowds, taking no precautions, and sooner or later a bullet would find him—then he and his daughter would know who had been right all along.

Starbuck stirred restlessly, sighed. What the hell! He was only fooling himself. He could no more let that happen than he could walk to the moon. He'd taken on the chore of looking out for Orville Flood, and whether or not he liked him personally he'd have to live with it. But he'd say nothing to Flood; let him send his telegram to Santa Fe and get the refusal that was certain to come back; things might go a bit smoother after that.

"You ready to chow down some?"

Frank Ogden's voice broke into his thoughts. He looked up. The old driver was standing at the edge of the gallery. Shawn nodded to him.

"I am, but I'm waiting on the Floods. Like to see them inside first."

"They're coming now," Ogden said, ducking his head at the door of the hotel. "Looks like they've got some of the big muckety-mucks with them."

Shawn made no comment as he watched Flood and Carla, accompanied by three well-dressed men—one of whom was probably the mayor, he supposed—move out onto the porch, cross in front of him without any sign of recognition, and enter the restaurant. A few of the passersby had slowed their steps, smiled, and spoken to the man, all drawing Starbuck's sharp attention, but to his relief Flood had not stopped.

When the party had disappeared into the building, Shawn drew himself upright, and nodding to Frank Ogden, followed. Noting with satisfaction that Flood and the others were choosing a large table in the center of the room, he led the way to one placed against the wall, from which he had a good view of not only the street outside the window but of the doorway as well.

They ordered their meal from a primly dressed waitress and sat back to wait. Ogden, tamping tobacco into the charred bowl of a blackened pipe, waited while the returning waitress set cups of coffee before them, and then spoke. "You meet the law here yet?"

"Nope. Figure to after we've eaten."

"This here's the county seat," the driver continued. "Done a little prying down at the livery stable. They got a sheriff name of Bert Wilger. Mighty well thought of, seems."

"Thought maybe he'd show up at the hotel when we came in."

"Out somewheres doing something. Deputy of

his is running things. Name's Jess Carr. Way the hostler talked, he's mighty busy showing off. . . . Wilger's due back afore dark."

The waitress appeared, bringing the food that had been ordered. She served them silently, then hurried back to the kitchen. A second girl was busy at the Flood table.

"Vittles sure smell good," Ogden commented, putting aside his pipe and taking up a knife and fork. "I'm pretty hungry."

Shawn turned to his plate. He ate slowly, with little interest. Outside in the street traffic was increasing. New customers entered the restaurant, others departed. Somewhere in the town a church bell tolled in measured beats. A buggy sped by in a great hurry, its iron wheels grating through the sandy soil.

He glanced at the table where the Floods and their three guests, or hosts, whichever it was, were seated. All but Carla were looking at him. Orville was speaking, and the trio of local officials, their faces set and disapproving, were apparently being made aware of what Flood believed was unnecessary and unwarranted interference. Starbuck nodded coolly, whereupon the men turned away quickly.

"You hanging around till they're done?" Ogden asked, pushing back his plate.

Shawn, a ghost of a smile on his lips, nodded. "Expect I'd better. You go on."

The driver got to his feet stiffly. "Reckon I'll do that. Bones of mine are complaining a-plenty. See you up in the room."

Starbuck beckoned to the waitress for a refill of his coffee cup. He watched Ogden thump toward the door, the man's spare, bent figure betraying his years. Frank was too old for the job he'd undertaken, there was no doubt of that. Each night Shawn had noticed how increasingly worn the driver was. Evidently he had been in dire need of work. . . . Suddenly his thoughts halted abruptly.

The Flood party had finished their meal, were rising and moving toward the doorway. Shawn laid enough money on the table to take care of his and Frank Ogden's check, and followed them out onto the walk, keeping well back in the shadows where he would be unseen. Carla and the men paused in front of the hotel. There was a round of handshakes and good nights, and then the local officials moved on. Flood and his daughter turned into the Western Star.

Starbuck crossed to the entrance of the hostelry, waited while the pair mounted the stairs and gained the upper hall. Entering, he stood at the foot of the steps until he heard their doors close. A sigh slipped from his lips at that. They had gotten through another day, and now, in their beds, within locked rooms, they were safe. He swung about, faced the clerk at his desk. "Where'll I find the sheriff's office?"

Quinn's brows lifted. "Out front, cut right," he said. "Be about fifty yards down the street. Something wrong?"

"No," Shawn replied, and returned to the sidewalk.

He came to a quick stop. Directly opposite, a man was standing in the mouth of the passageway that separated two buildings. Even in the shadows there was no mistaking the fancy Mexican trappings of silver, the peaked hat with its wide, rolled brim. It was Cruz Mendoza.

At once the vaquero faded back into the narrow alley. Starbuck came off the hotel porch quickly and started across the now uncrowded street. Mendoza had been watching Flood, there was no doubt of that. Reaching the opening between the adjacent structures, Shawn halted. The Mexican had disappeared. He hurried on to the far end of the passage, drew up in the alley. Mendoza was not in sight.

Stepping up against the corner of the nearest building, he waited, listening and watching, but after a full five minutes he turned and made his way back to the street. It would be useless to hunt for Mendoza in the dark—and in a strange town—and if he did catch him, there was little he could do. The man had committed no crime, could not even be accused of having made any threats upon Orville Flood's life.

And it was possible Mendoza meant no harm, although his actions back on the road certainly made him suspect. Regardless, he would bear close watching that next day when Flood made his appearance on the speaker's stand, Shawn realized as he bent his steps toward the sheriff's office. He'd best be considered in the same light as the man in the tattered hat.

He drew abreast the lawman's quarters, stepped through the doorway into the well-lighted office. At the desk was a man somewhere in his early fifties, round-faced, and with stern, unwavering eyes. This would be the sheriff, Bert Wilger. Slouched in a chair beyond him, toying with a silver-plated pistol, was a much younger man. Jess Carr, the deputy, Shawn supposed.

Wilger glanced up from the stack of wanted posters through which he was thumbing. "Something I can do for you?"

Starbuck introduced himself, shook hands with both men, and explained his purpose in Bonnerville, finishing with a request that a half a dozen or so extra deputies be sworn in and scattered about through the large crowd that was sure to be in attendance.

"Been giving that some thought," Wilger said. "Some of the folks I've run into seem a bit riled."

Shawn nodded. "Not so afraid of them. Usually about all they do is talk loud, maybe call Flood a liar or a crook. There's one for sure—maybe more—that's out to kill him."

Wilger leaned forward, placed his elbows on his desk. Jess Carr straightened up in his chair, interest showing on his lean features.

"Kill him—you sure of that?" the sheriff asked.

"Tried today, in San Ignacio. Spotted him on the roof of a store just in time, drove him off."

"You get a good look at him?" Carr wondered.

"No. Only description I can give you is that he's wearing a hat with a brim that's ragged, and he was carrying a rifle."

"Not much to go on," Wilger muttered, "but we'll be on the lookout. Anybody else?"

"There's a vaquero. Ran into him on the road this afternoon. Spotted him a few minutes ago down the street. Don't know anything for sure about him except he's got me worrying some. Calls himself Cruz Mendoza."

Wilger gave that thought, shook his head. "Name ain't familiar to me. You know him, Jess?" he asked, turning to the deputy.

Carr shrugged. "Town's full of strangers."

"For a fact," Wilger agreed, rising. "I'll see you get your deputies. Now, it's been a long day. Was about to turn in but I'm needing a drink first. You care to join me?"

"Be my pleasure, Sheriff," Starbuck replied, and followed the older man out onto the walk. "Wanted to ask you something else. Man by the name of Damon Friend—you ever run across him?"

"Friend," Wilger repeated slowly. "No, can't say as the name's familiar. Why?"

"Been looking for him. Thought he might have come through here. Would probably've put on a boxing match—"

The muffled rap of two quick gunshots echoed along the street. Wilger and Starbuck wheeled together, glancing toward the scatter of persons still abroad in the night who began to hurry toward the Western Star. Jess Carr came from inside the jail.

"Where'd them shots come from?"

"The hotel," Starbuck answered in a tight voice, and not waiting to see if the lawmen followed, broke into a run for the structure.

6

Starbuck pushed his way through the crowd of people jamming the entrance to the hotel. Ignoring their angry protests, he drove a path to the door and into the lobby. His first glimpse was of Frank Ogden. The driver, clad only in undershirt and pants, bootless, was coming toward him. A pistol was in his hand.

"It was him!" he shouted. "That yahoo with the chewed up hat you seen in San Ignacio! Was trying to get into Flood's room—"

"They all right?" Shawn asked quickly, gripping the older man by the arms in an effort to calm him.

"Sure . . . sure . . . I'd just turned in. Heard a door rattling, figured it was you. Got up to let you in, but when I looked out into the hall, there he was at Flood's door trying to bust it open. He gave me a look and started off down the hall. I grabbed my gun, took a couple of shots at him."

"You think you hit him?"

Shawn glanced at the man asking the question. It was Sheriff Wilger. Next to him was Carr, his deputy. He hadn't noticed them following him into the building.

"Ain't sure. Was plenty dark."

"There's a door at that end of the hall," Carr said. "Lets out into the alley."

Wilger wheeled at once to Shawn. "You and your friend take a look in the empty rooms up here. Jess and me'll get outside, close off the alley. Maybe we can still trap him."

The two lawmen cut back through the crowd to the street. Starbuck, followed closely by Frank Ogden, mounted the stairs at a run. When they reached Flood's room, Shawn halted, rapped sharply on the scarred door.

Orville Flood's voice, strained and uncertain, said, "Yes? Who is it?"

"Starbuck," Shawn replied. "Keep locked up— and stay away from the windows. Understand?"

"Yes—"

Shawn continued on down the hall, trying the doors in turn as he came to them. All were locked. With Ogden at his side he reached the end of the corridor.

"Want you to wait here," he said to the old driver. "Odds are that jasper made it to the alley, but we won't take any chances. You keep an eye on the hall just in case he ducked into one of the rooms. You see him come out, you know what to do."

Ogden bobbed his head vigorously. "For sure. Where'll you be?"

"I'm going out the back—"

Shawn pivoted to the door at the end of the hall, stepped out onto a small landing. Below, and to his left, he could hear someone moving slowly along the hard-baked ground. Immediately his hand dropped to the weapon hanging on his hip, then slid away as Wilger's voice came to him.

"Starbuck?"

"Right," Shawn answered, and hurriedly descended the steep flight of stairs. "No luck in the hall."

"Figured that. He wouldn't hang around in there once your friend started shooting. He's out here somewhere."

"Where's your deputy?" Starbuck asked as they moved slowly along the alley.

Wilger halted to look inside a shed, found it empty, resumed his position. "Up ahead—working toward us. Reckon there's no doubt he's the man that you saw back at San Ignacio."

"He's the same, according to Ogden. Got to run him down, else I'll be forced to make Flood call off the debate tomorrow."

"I'll back you up there. Be setting himself up for a bullet if he gets up on that stand."

Shawn grinned wryly as they pressed quietly and deliberately along through the half dark. He could easily imagine the Floods' reaction should he have to make that decision. And Carla—he smiled again thinking of what she would say. But they shouldn't question the wisdom of such a move; the killer's attempt to enter Orville Flood's room ought to be proof enough that he was in danger.

"That you, Bert?"

It was the deputy. His call came from the deep shadows off to the left of the alley.

"Yeh," Wilger answered. "Got Starbuck with me. You see anything?"

"Nothing, but there's a lot of boxes and stuff. Looked through them best I could but just might've passed him up. There's a hell of a lot of places where he could've hid."

"We'll double back over your tracks then," the sheriff said. "Three of us hunting ain't going to miss him."

"Kept his horse handy in San Ignacio," Shawn said. "Could have done the same here."

"Doubt it. We got out here fast and we'd've heard him leaving. Pretty quiet around here right now."

Starbuck admitted to that. Only faint sounds were rising from the street lying beyond the buildings to their right—the tinkling of a piano in some saloon, an occasional shout or burst of laughter. Bonnerville had fairly well settled down for the night.

They resumed the search, working three abreast slowly, examining every possible place that could afford a hiding place for the would-be killer, and turned up nothing. Reaching the end of the alley, Bert Wilger swore quietly, shook his head. "Hate to say it, but he's plumb got away from us."

"Means we'll sure have to watch for him tomorrow," Carr said.

"It's now that's worrying me," Starbuck murmured. "With him running loose there's nothing to keep him from trying again."

"What I was thinking," Wilger agreed. "I figure we ought to set up a watch over your man."

Shawn nodded. "Just what I aim to do—"

"What *we'll* do," the sheriff corrected. "There's three of us. We can break it up into three shifts. You take the first—say till midnight. Me and Jess'll handle the rest of the night."

"I'll be obliged to you," Starbuck said, smiling. "Have to admit I'm beat, and my partner's real done in."

"Then it's settled. You fix it up with Flood so's he'll know what's going on and who we are. . . . If that bird shows up again, one of us'll be there to hand him a hot welcome."

7

Starbuck awoke shortly before dawn. Ogden was already up, sitting on the edge of the lumpy bed rubbing at the stiff stubble that clothed his chin. He turned, grinned at Shawn.

"Morning . . . Reckon I'd best rustle me up a shave today or the kids'll be taking me for Santy Claus."

"Help yourself to my soap and razor," Starbuck said, rising and starting to dress. "Find it there on the washstand."

"Obliged to you," Ogden replied, "but I got my own. Anyways, I think I'll treat myself to some fancy barbering and a squirt or two of that sweet-smelling lilac water down the street. Shaving's something I'd rather take a beating than do."

While the driver drew on his clothing, Shawn examined his reflection in the wavey mirror. He could get by without using the blade and lather, he decided—at least until later in the day.

"We eating first off?" Ogden asked.

Starbuck nodded. "Might as well. Don't expect the Floods will be up and about for a couple hours yet. You ready?"

"Ready as I'll ever be," the old driver said, and moved to the door.

He opened the panel, stepped out into the hall.

Starbuck, close behind him, frowned, came to a halt. The corridor was deserted. He had expected either Carr or Bert Wilger to be in the chair placed in front of the Floods' quarters.

"What's wrong?" Ogden asked.

"Like I mentioned last night, the sheriff, his deputy, and me stood watch. Figured one of them would be here now."

Ogden shrugged. "Prob'ly hung around till daylight, then went home, figuring it wasn't no use staying any longer."

It was a reasonable explanation, Shawn agreed, and stepping to Flood's door placed his ear against the flimsy panel. All was quiet inside the room. Apparently Orville was still asleep.

"Seems all right," he said, and following the driver to the stairway, descended to the lobby.

Two men and a small boy occupied three of the leather chairs, evidently on hand early for the day's festivities. Quinn, the clerk, looked up from a newspaper he was reading, nodded automatically to them as they moved by his desk.

Stepping out onto the gallery, they turned to the restaurant and entered, finding it with only a few patrons at so early an hour. Taking the same table as the night before, they settled down to a hearty breakfast of meat, potatoes, and coffee, and a short time later were again on the sidewalk.

"Expect I'd better see to the horses," Ogden said, again giving his whiskers a thorough rubbing. "Didn't think much of that hostler at the stable. If he didn't give them animals a good currying like I told him, I aim to dress him down good. Where you headed?"

"Got to find Wilger, get those extra deputies lined up," Starbuck replied. "See you later."

He swung off down the street in the direction of the lawman's office. A few people were beginning to appear along the walks now, and two men were busy arranging a row of chairs on the platform where the dignitaries were to sit during the debate. Another was repairing the bunting draped across its front, torn loose, somehow, during the night. A small group of men stood off to one side in earnest conversation. Several had signs, and it would seem the formation of a parade was about to get under way.

He reached Wilger's office. The door was closed but unlocked and he entered. There was no one there. He stood in the center of the room considering what next to do; he had no idea where Bert Wilger lived—undoubtedly in one of the houses that lay outside the business area. Carr, too, likely would have a home in that section of the settlement, and both could be catching up on their sleep after spending the night watching over the Floods.

There was another possibility; either one or both could be having breakfast in one of the other cafés. He returned to the street, made a tour of its length, looking into the several restaurants he encountered as well as into Hap's Saloon, already open and doing business, but there was no sign of either Wilger or Carr. Once more on the sidewalk, and noting a man sweeping the dust from the landing in front of his store, he crossed to him.

"You tell me where Bert Wilger lives?"

The merchant paused, leaned on his broom. "You needing the sheriff for something?"

"Hardly be looking for him if I didn't want to see him," Starbuck replied, irritated. A vague uneasiness was beginning to build within him. If the lawman or his deputy, whichever had taken the last shift of the watch, had left the hotel at daylight, it was only reasonable to think he would still be somewhere along the street. He would certainly take his meal before going to bed.

"Was just asking," the storekeeper said, unperturbed. "He's got hisself a place over back of the jail. Brown house with a white board fence. You go straight down the—"

"I'll find it," Starbuck said, moving on. "Obliged to you."

The unaccountable disturbance within him continued to grow. He tried to analyze his feelings, the restless anxiety that was troubling him, and came up with the thought that it could only have to do with the events of the preceding night and what he would face in the coming day. It was to be expected, he supposed, but it shouldn't be too bad; he had Wilger's promise of several deputies to help him keep an eye on the crowd.

He reached the jail, circled to the alley behind, and found the house described by the merchant. Wilger was not there. A horse was in the barn at the rear of the lot; two saddles and other gear were on racks and hanging from pegs in the wall. The lawman was in town; Shawn took some satisfaction from that.

Wheeling about, he started for the hotel. He would see the lawman later—there was still plenty of time before the meeting and debate got under way. Best he see to the Floods, get them down for their morning meal—he intended to ride close herd over them until the affair was over and they were safely gone from Bonnerville. After they had eaten and they were again in their rooms, he'd look again for Wilger.

He entered the Western Star by the back stairway, having made his approach from the alley, walked the length of the hallway, and halted at Orville Flood's door. He listened briefly, and hearing nothing, he rapped sharply. Ordinarily the Floods rose early, but after the previous night's excitement he guessed they were sleeping in.

There was no answer to his knock. He repeated it—again no reply. Frowning, anxiety once more gripping him, Shawn reached for the china knob, turned it. The door opened. It had not been locked. Suddenly filled with alarm, Starbuck drew his gun and stepped into the room. He pulled up short.

Sheriff Wilger lay face down on the floor, a broad stain of dried blood on his back. There was no sign of Orville Flood. Grim, Shawn crossed to the doorway leading into the adjoining room occupied by Carla. The girl, too, was gone.

He turned back to the lawman, knelt beside him. Perhaps he was still alive, could give him some idea of what had happened. He saw he would get no help from Bert Wilger. A knife had been thrust deep into the lawman's body, bringing a quick death. Two furrows scuffed into the cheap carpeting indicated he had been murdered in the hallway and dragged into the room.

Starbuck drew himself upright, began a circuit of the room searching for something— for anything that would answer the questions crowding into his mind. An envelope lying on the table near the window caught his eye. He crossed to it, saw that it had his name written upon it. Snatching it up he ripped it open, took out the sheet of paper it contained, and unfolded it. His face hardened and a curse slipped from his lips as he read it. Orville and Carla Flood had been kidnapped.

8

Taut, Starbuck read the note through for a second time:

> We've got Flood and the girl. Ride north on the Blackman Trail soon as you get this. Don't tell anybody and come alone. You'll be watched.

Shawn crushed the note in his hand, thrust it into his pocket, anger, fear, and frustration all mingling and having their way with him. It was unbelievable that it could have happened—that he had not been aware of any disturbance; he had been sleeping no more than thirty feet away from where Wilger had been murdered! And surely the Floods had put up a struggle of some kind when they were being taken out!

But that was all past now, and nothing could be done about it. The two were in the hands of ruthless killers, one of whom, to judge from the handwriting in the letter, was fairly well educated. He had no choice but to do as he was ordered.

There was a light knock at the doorway. Shawn, nerves honed razor sharp, pivoted hurriedly. Ernie Quinn, the hotel clerk, was standing in the opening.

"Heard somebody pounding—" he began, and then choked as his eyes fell upon Wilger's body. "That—that the sheriff?"

"Come inside," Starbuck snapped, silently cursing himself for not closing the door earlier. He waited until the man had entered, glance still fixed upon the lawman, reached past him, and pushed the panel shut.

"Was it—did you kill him?"

"You know better than that!" Starbuck snarled. "I came in here to see Flood, found the sheriff there on the floor."

He hesitated, debating with himself the advisability of taking Quinn into his confidence. The note had warned him to tell no one of what had occurred but he had to get word to Frank Ogden and Deputy Jess Carr, and there was no time to hunt them down. There was a deadly urgency to the instructions he'd received, and the sooner he followed out the orders given him, the better for the Floods. He would have to rely on the hotel's clerk.

Reaching out, he grasped Quinn by the arm. The man flinched, pulled back, but Starbuck did not slacken his grip.

"You're to keep your mouth shut about this, hear?"

Quinn nodded frantically.

"Now, listen close to me. The Floods have been kidnapped. Men who did it left a note for me, telling me what I've got to do—alone."

"Alone?" the clerk echoed. "Why don't you get a posse and—"

"Note warned me not to, and if I try it, I'll probably get the Floods killed. Now, I want you to lock this room so nobody can get in here. Then I want you to find Jess Carr and Frank Ogden, tell them what happened—but warn them not to try and follow me. Carr will know what to do about the sheriff's body."

Quinn appeared to have recovered himself somewhat. He nodded his understanding, said, "What about the debate? People are going to be asking questions. . . ."

"That's a job for Ogden. Tell him I said to go see the mayor, or whoever's in charge of the thing, and say that Flood's sick or something, that the meeting with Josson will have to be postponed—"

"Whyn't you just tell them there's been a kidnapping?"

"Because I don't want a bunch of trigger-happy heroes taking it on themselves to start looking for Flood and his daughter and making things worse for them!" Shawn said, moving toward the door. "Got a hunch this is going to be plenty touchy as it is."

He halted, hand on the door knob, waiting for Quinn to follow. The room clerk was again studying the body of Bert Wilger, a frown on his face.

"Something I ain't understanding," he said doubtfully. "Was your job to be looking out for the Floods, so what's the sheriff doing here?"

"After that jasper tried to break in here last night, we figured it best to stand guard—Wilger, Carr, and me. I was out there in the hall early. Carr relieved me, and the sheriff took over from him. The kidnapping—and the murder—took place while he was on the job."

"Sure don't seem right, somehow—"

"The hell with that!" Starbuck said impatiently. "You can thresh it out with Carr when you see him. I've got to get moving—and before I go I want to see you lock this door."

Quinn stepped by him into the hall, pulled the panel shut, and turned the lock with his passkey. He came about, faced Shawn uncertainly.

"You said for me first to—"

"Go find Jess Carr," Starbuck said wearily. "Tell him what I told you, then hunt up Ogden—and keep your mouth shut to everybody else."

The clerk wheeled, headed down the stairway. Shawn made a brief check of his cartridge belt, saw that most all of the loops were filled, and followed. He could only hope he would encounter Carr and Ogden himself as he went for his horse and lay it all out before them personally; it was doubtful Ernie Quinn could remember all he'd been told to do but time was short and he had no choice but to take a chance on the man.

Reaching the sidewalk, he caught a glimpse of Quinn turning right and legging it for the jail. Swinging into the opposite direction, Shawn hurried toward the livery stable. It was still fairly early and crowds had not yet begun to collect in the street, he noticed, but it wouldn't be long before the town square would fill. There'd be a howl go up when Orville Flood failed to put in an appearance—and the day certainly would be won by his opponent, Tom Josson.

He came to the stable, trotted through the wide doors, both standing open to admit the fresh, warm sunlight. The hostler heard the rap of his boot heels and emerged lazily from the littered office that fronted the runway.

"You wanting something?"

"My horse," Starbuck replied, not breaking stride. He glanced about, still hopeful of finding Frank Ogden passing the time by working with his team or repairing a harness. "My partner—you seen him this morning?"

"Was here, early," the stableman said, moving in beside Shawn. "Borrowed a saddle and horse. Had a hankering to take a ride, so he claimed. Was heading toward the river when he left here. Why—there something wrong?"

"No," Starbuck answered, turning into the stall where the sorrel was quartered. At once he began to throw his gear onto the big gelding. "He comes in, tell him to go talk to Ernie Quinn."

"That hotel clerk fellow?"

"Yeah. Left a message with him for Frank."

The sorrel was ready. Shawn backed him out of the stall, swung onto the saddle. Wheeling about, he looked at the hostler. "How do I get on the Blackman Trail?"

"The Blackman?" the man repeated in surprise. "It don't go nowheres since the landslide. Just runs flat up against the mountain. You must be meaning some other—"

"No, it's the one I'm looking for."

The stableman shrugged. "Well, I reckon you know what you want. Follow the road north out of town. When you come to the forks, take the right hand."

"Obliged," Starbuck said, and raked the sorrel lightly with his rowels.

Moving the length of the runway, he broke out into the open, slowed as a gathering of people in front of the jail down the street caught his attention. He squinted against the sun, focused his eyes on a man standing a bit apart on the sidewalk, facing the crowd. It was Ernie Quinn.

Anger whipped through Starbuck as he realized what was happening. The clerk, evidently unable to contain his sudden importance and hoping for further prominence, was doing just what he'd been warned not to do—telling all within range of his voice of the kidnappings and of the murder of Sheriff Bert Wilger.

The damned fool! Couldn't he see what would result? Every man in town would grab a gun, mount a horse, and become a self-appointed lawman, out to track down the criminals—the very thing he'd been cautioned against in the note.

A quick burst of yells echoed along the street. Starbuck stiffened. The crowd was shifting, starting to move in his direction.

"There he is!" a voice shouted.

Immediately gunshots crackled through the warm air. Dust spurted up from the roadway a short distance beyond him.

Shawn swore feelingly. Quinn was somehow connecting him with the crimes—likely was blaming him for the death of Wilger! Jamming his spurs into the sorrel's flanks, he cut the big gelding about sharply and sent him racing across the field for the road.

9

A quarter mile later, as the sorrel pounded along the well-traveled route leading northward from town, Starbuck glanced over his shoulder. There were no signs of pursuit as yet, and he eased up on the big horse, allowing him to settle into a fair lope.

It would take several minutes for the posse to get mounted, and by the time it was well under way he, hopefully, would have reached the forks and turned off, leaving them to continue on the main road—but that too was something to be hoped for. If any member of the posse took the precaution of questioning the hostler at the livery stable, they would know he planned to swing off onto the Blackman Trail, which would bring further complications. Shawn shrugged at the possibility. If it worked out that way there was nothing he could do about it; he would simply have to face the problem when it presented itself.

He should have known better than to rely on Ernie Quinn—just as he now felt a sense of blame in that he had shifted some of his responsibility for the Floods to Bert Wilger and Jess Carr. He should have been there in the hallway of the hotel standing guard, not two outsiders whose interest did not go beyond their ordinary duty. Like as not, Wilger, tired after a long day, had fallen asleep in the chair and made things easy for the outlaws.

Starbuck looked ahead. The branch in the road was at hand, and once more he threw a glance to his back trail. The posse was not in sight but he did not veer immediately onto the turnoff. He continued on for a short distance and then cut back, rejoining it farther on. Anyone following the tracks of the sorrel would find no indication that he had swung off onto the trail at the forks.

The road, slanting into the northeast toward a towering, pine-covered mountain, was one not often traveled. There were deep ruts indicating that once it had been a popular route, but now brush crowded in on both sides and grass grew thick in the wheel marks as if anxious to hide the scars left by passing pilgrims.

Shawn rode steadily on. He was following blindly the instructions given him in the note by the outlaws and could only hope that no harm had as yet befallen the Floods. Undoubtedly they had been kidnapped for ransom, and if so the chances were good they could be brought through the ordeal once the necessary amount of money was paid.

He frowned, felt a stir of worry; what if it wasn't money the kidnappers wanted? What if they were interested only in removing Orville Flood from the political scene? If true, then he could expect the worst for both Flood and his daughter. . . . But that didn't seem logical. They would hardly have left a note for him if that was what they had in mind.

Two hours later he was well into a scatter of small, brushy foothills that lay at the base of the mountain, following out a path in a narrow, sandy-floored arroyo that bore directly for a distant ridge. Evidently there was a pass through the higher country and the rocky hogback he could see silhouetted against the sky. The hostler, however, had spoken of a landslide and implied that it had closed the Blackman Trail; if so he should shortly come to the end of the route.

He was speculating upon that when, abruptly, two riders broke from the brush to either side and confronted him. Their appearance was so unexpected that it brought the sorrel to his hind legs and sent Starbuck reaching for his weapon. His hand fell away as he recognized the man to his left, Cruz Mendoza, and saw the vaquero's pistol and that of his partner leveled at him.

"*Buenos dias, senor,*" the Mexican said when the sorrel had quieted. "We meet again, eh?"

Shawn studied the vaquero in silence. That day before when he had stopped them on the road it apparently had been to make certain Orville Flood was a passenger in the coach. On the street that previous night he had been locating the room the Floods occupied in the hotel.

"There is no need for anger," Mendoza said, smiling and waggling the silvered, ornate weapon he was holding.

"It is simply a matter of business, amigo. . . . Now I would have you meet my *compadre*, Lonnie Frick."

Frick was a husky, blond man of about his own age, Shawn saw. He had a knife scar that traced down one side of his face.

"We have watched you many miles," Mendoza said as the blond man moved in behind Starbuck, relieved him of his weapon. "You are wise to come alone."

"Did what the note told me to," Shawn said quietly. "Where's the Floods?"

"In time you will see them. Be of patience."

"Have they been hurt?"

The vaquero assumed a pained expression. "I assure you, senor, they have not been harmed. Our fat rabbit is of too great a value to injure."

Starbuck breathed a little easier. "Then it's money you're after?"

"Of course," Mendoza said with an exaggerated shrug of his shoulders. His thick brows lifted as Shawn's meaning became clear to him. "You think it was for this politics thing? Ha! That is a joke, senor. We care nothing for your politics—only for the money your rich *patrons* will pay to get back their *tonto*."

The word was lost to Shawn but was one

he assumed had to do with Flood being the representative of the party in Santa Fe. He started to question more, but Frick, moving about impatiently, spoke up.

"Let's cut out the yammering and get moving," he said. "Cole and the others'll be on the yonder side of the mountain if we don't get cracking."

"You are right, amigo," Mendoza said in his elaborate, polite manner. "We must ride. I will go with our prisoner. You follow—it is best we watch the trail. A posse could be coming."

Frick shifted his hard-eyed glance to Starbuck. "What about it, mister? There any chance of that?"

Starbuck met the outlaw's cold stare evenly. "I did what the note told me to. If there's a posse it's somebody else's doing, not mine."

"You are wise," the vaquero murmured, "still, you will watch close, Lonnie."

Frick wheeled about, dropped back fifty yards or so. Mendoza motioned to the trail.

"Ride, senor, and you will please try no tricks. I would regret shooting you."

"Doubt if you'd do that," Shawn said, moving out ahead of the vaquero. "I must be important to your plan, else you wouldn't have gone to all the trouble to bring me out here."

"*Si*, it is agreed, but with an arm broken by a bullet a man can still be useful—"

"Cruz!" Frick's voice reached them suddenly.

"Riders are coming! It's a posse, sure'er'n hell!"

Starbuck stirred wearily. He was having no luck. The men from town had apparently questioned the hostler at the stable and learned that he would be taking the Blackman Trail. He glanced up as the vaquero rode in close, his eyes dark and angry. Mendoza studied him for a long breath, and then shrugged.

"I think this is not of your making, for as I have said, you are too wise." He dropped back a few paces, waved to Frick. "The high trail, amigo!" he called. "We will lose them there."

Immediately Lonnie cut away from the arroyo and began to climb the slope. Mendoza nodded at Starbuck, motioned toward the hogback.

"You will start. I do not think you want to meet them any more than I do."

Shawn wheeled the sorrel broadside to the slope, dug spurs into his flanks, and sent him scrambling up the steep grade. Mendoza followed, keeping a bit to one side in order to avoid the cascading gravel dislodged by the gelding's hooves.

A quarter hour later they were on a rocky bench considerably higher than the trail and moving along at a good pace. Starbuck glanced at the land below. The posse, fifteen or twenty men, was clearly visible.

"Soon they will be gone," the vaquero said. "And with darkness they will turn back for town, all very tired and in need of whiskey. Is it that they seek us because of Orville Flood or because their sheriff was killed?"

"Both, maybe, but I expect they want me most of all. They've got it in their head that I murdered Wilger."

"Why? Such is foolishness—"

"The hotel clerk found me in the room with the body. Had a hunch then he was making up his mind that I did it."

"Ah, yes, the one named Quinn," Mendoza said, shaking his head sympathetically. "It is unfortunate when one must deal with a fool—but we are here, senor. We have caught up with my friends—and yours. . . . I am sure they will be happy to see you."

10

There was a spring wagon with a stained canvas stretched over the bed and held taut with wooden bows. Branches had been torn from bushes and small trees and affixed here and there to complete the camouflage job. The kidnappers had planned carefully; instead of holding their prisoners captive in a cabin or some such stationary point, they could move about and thereby afford little opportunity for rescue.

Two men came from the brush into which the wagon had been pulled. One was a squat, barrel-chested individual wearing a fringed, buckskin coat. The other was small, lean, with a quiet manner and cold, gray eyes. He was fairly well dressed and could easily be mistaken for a successful businessman.

Looking on beyond them, Starbuck saw Carla Flood appear at the end of the wagon. Relief spread across her strained features. She turned, said something over her shoulder. Almost immediately Orville Flood was moving past her and climbing down from the vehicle.

"Was a posse coming behind him, Cole," Frick announced as they rode into the small clearing and dismounted.

The features of the small man hardened. He

placed his attention on Shawn. "I warned you to come alone," he said in a cold voice.

"I did," Starbuck snapped. "Was their idea to follow me, not mine."

"This I believe," Mendoza murmured. "This posse, it thinks that he killed the sheriff."

As Cole considered that idea, no expression crossed his narrow features. Then, "Where is it now?"

"In the small hills below. We take the high trail and they do not see us but pass on by."

Cole's shoulders relaxed slightly. "All right, we'll say it was not your fault," he said, and glanced up as Flood, sweating profusely, stepped in beside him. Shawn looked at the man closely.

"You and your daughter all right?"

Flood nodded. "Much as we can be. Was beginning to think you weren't coming."

"Moved as fast as I could after I found that letter," Shawn replied. "What's this all about?"

"They're holding me for ransom," Flood said. "Whether I—and my daughter—live depends on you."

Starbuck frowned. "Me?"

The outlaw called Cole folded his arms across his chest and said, "That's right—on you, mister." He bucked his head at the man in the fringed coat. "Ed, get those horses out of sight while I do some explaining."

Ed turned, gathered in the reins of the sorrel

and the mounts Mendoza and Frick had been riding, and started off toward the brush. Carla had come down from the wagon, Shawn noticed, and was now standing at the rear of it watching him intently. Her hair was disarranged, had been hastily pinned up in haphazard fashion. She was wearing the dove-gray suit he had seen on her before, and while it showed streaks of dirt and what looked to be a smear of grease on the lower part of the skirt, she appeared to be no worse for wear otherwise.

"Just to keep things straight," Cole said, "I'm the man that's running this show. Name's Cole Lester. You already know Mendoza, there, and Lonnie. Ed Jacks is the gentleman taking care of your horse."

Starbuck made no comment as he waited for the outlaw to continue. That Lester was a cut above his partners was easy to see.

"Get to the point," Flood said peevishly. "Sooner he gets started, the sooner he'll be back."

"You're right as usual, Orville," Cole said drily. "It's just that I want everything understood."

"What's there to understand?" Flood demanded in an outraged voice. "You're holding us for ransom! That's all there is to it—and I'll tell you this, you'll not get away with it—never!"

"We will," Cole Lester said calmly. "I know just how much you're worth to your brother and his friends. They know they'll never put over that

Pastizal deal unless you're elected—so they've got to have you. That puts me in the driver's seat."

"You're fools—all of you! Fools to try this."

"Fools get away with such things, senor," Cruz Mendoza said, "because they are foolish enough to try."

Ed Jacks, his chore of hiding the horses completed, returned to the clearing. Squatting on his heels, he began to roll a cigarette. The vaquero hunched down beside him, reached out a brown hand for the sack of tobacco and sheaf of papers. Lonnie Frick lolled against a bulge of rock, eyes on Carla. Somewhere up near the ridge a squirrel scolded.

"You're to be our messenger," Lester said, breaking the hush. "You'll carry a letter to Flood's brother for us."

"The ransom note—"

"Exactly. It goes to Carl Flood. You'll wait while he gets the money and then bring it back to us."

"How much money?"

Cole Lester shrugged. "Not that it has any bearing on your part of the plan, but it will be fifty thousand dollars."

Starbuck considered that doubtfully. "A lot of money. You think he can raise that much?"

"He will. You underestimate the worth of Orville to the committee. They've got to have him."

"Don't you worry about Carl paying off!" Flood said confidently. "He won't leave me—us—here to die. Family means more to him than that."

Lester touched Flood with a sardonic look. "Doubt if that's the reason he'll come across, but we won't go into it." He paused, glanced at Shawn. "You have any objections?"

"Of course he hasn't!" Flood shouted. "Was hired to look out for me, wasn't he? This is part of the job."

"Guess that answers for me," Starbuck said. "After I get the money where do I meet you—here?"

"No, we'll be on the move," Lester said. "An hour after you pull out, we'll be gone from here. By tomorrow we may be ten miles north or five to the south, all depending on my fancy. . . . That's our insurance against your sending somebody like a company of soldiers in after us, not that I think you'd be fool enough to try."

"I'll keep to the deal."

"You do that and everything'll go fine for Orville and the girl. Now, when you get the money just head back this way. Mendoza and Lonnie'll be waiting. They'll find you—you don't have to worry about finding them. All you do is ride—that clear?"

Shawn nodded. It was to be the same as before; the outlaws would watch him, keep close tabs on him until they were certain he was unaccompanied and up to no tricks, then they would appear.

"Just one word of warning," Cole Lester said. "Don't try anything, like setting up a trap while you're in Santa Fe. We'll know every move you make, and if you—"

"No danger of that," Shawn cut in. "Now let me give you a bit of advice. Intend to do what I'm told, but if anything happens to either of these people while I'm gone—the slightest thing—you'll answer to me."

"You've got my word they'll not be harmed," Lester said coolly. "I guarantee that same as I guarantee we'll kill them if you don't bring the money. Want you to make Carl Flood understand that. We've gone this far, we've got nothing to lose."

"You can forget that," Starbuck said quietly. "It won't be their fault if I don't get it—and killing them will put me and every lawman I can get to on your trail until you're caught and swinging from a gallows. . . . You got the ransom note?"

The outlaw reached into an inside pocket, produced a sealed envelope. He handed it to Shawn.

"This tells Carl Flood all he needs to know. It was written by Orville so he'll know it's genuine."

Starbuck tucked the letter inside his shirt. "How much time have I got?"

"Until sundown—Thursday."

Shawn stared at the outlaw. "That's cutting it plenty close."

"Should be no trouble for you. Sorrel of yours looks like a fine horse."

Starbuck started to protest further but realized it was probably useless. He turned to Mendoza. "How about my gun?"

The vaquero glanced at Lester. The outlaw chief nodded. "Give it to him. He'd be a fool to try using it."

Mendoza drew the weapon, given to him earlier by Frick, from his belt, and passed it butt first to Shawn. Holstering the pistol, Shawn started at once for the brush where the sorrel had been picketed. As he passed Orville Flood, the man grasped him by the arm.

"For God's sake—hurry!"

"Do the best I can," Starbuck replied, and nodding to Carla, continued on.

11

The sun was directly overhead when Shawn reached the foot of the mountain and broke out onto the flats. It was hot and the plains flowed out before him in endless, glittering miles, but he pushed the gelding to a fast pace. Cole Lester's deadline gave him little time to spare.

He would have preferred to swing wide, avoid cutting across open country; somewhere in the area the posse from Bonnerville still searched for him, and to encounter them would mean a costly delay at the least. But delay also would be incurred if he kept to the brush hillsides in the hope of remaining unseen since traveling would be much slower. He had weighed the matter carefully and had come finally to the conclusion that it was better to risk running into the posse and thus gain a few hours; if his luck proved bad and he was spotted by the men from Bonnerville, he'd simply depend on the speed of the big sorrel to carry him beyond their reach.

As the gelding loped tirelessly on, Starbuck began to think of the outlaws and to consider ways of outwitting them. It galled him to be forced into becoming a part of their plan; he'd been hired to protect the Floods, not participate in a blackmail scheme. He had failed both the men who had hired him and the Floods, it would seem.

But there was little he could do—at least for the time being. He didn't doubt that Cruz Mendoza and the scar-faced Lonnie Frick were somewhere in the area keeping an eye on him, and would continue to do so until he had returned with the ransom money. To attempt to bring back help could only mean trouble—probably death for Orville and Carla Flood.

He guessed there was nothing he could do but collect the money and carry it back, just as he'd been ordered to do. Then, once the cash was handed over to Cole Lester and his bunch and the Floods were safely out of their hands, he might be able to do something about the outlaws. He owed that much to the men who had hired him.

The afternoon wore on. At sundown he halted for a brief time to rest the sorrel and then continued, breaking again around midnight. Fortunately he had seen no signs of the Bonnerville posse and there had been no occasion to press the gelding beyond a steady lope.

He waited out a full hour, then once more mounted and resumed the grueling ride. He had made good time so far and he had hopes of maintaining the pace, but soon the sorrel began to slow as the long, upgrade miles to the settlement, perched on a plateau at the foot of the Sangre de Cristo mountains, took their toll of his strength.

And when the first fingers of yellow light began to spray up into the eastern sky, the big horse began to falter.

From that point on it was a matter of alternately riding and resting, of walking and leading the gelding, until they reached the town. Starbuck went first to a livery stable off the plaza with which he was familiar and saw to the care and feeding of the exhausted sorrel. That done, and ignoring his own needs, he returned to the business district and sought out the office of Carl Flood.

It proved to be both ornate and elaborate, and was located in one of Santa Fe's newer buildings, a short distance beyond the old Governor's Palace. Shawn, entering, came first into a reception room that was deserted. He crossed then into an inner door marked PRIVATE and knocked. A deep voice bade him enter.

Shawn had never met Carl Flood, his previous dealings being with one of the other members of the Central Party committee and the U.S. marshal, but he would have known him under any circumstances; he was a duplicate of his brother except that he appeared to be a few years older. He glanced up from the newspaper he was reading.

"Yes?"

Starbuck reached inside his shirt, produced Cole Lester's letter, and handing it to the man, waited for the reaction he knew was to come.

Carl Flood opened the envelope, spread the letter out on the table before him, and read it slowly, his face darkening with each passing moment. Abruptly he came to his feet.

"Of all the goddammed gall!" he shouted. "I'll see them in hell before I—" His words broke off as he turned his angry attention to Shawn. "You one of Lester's gang?"

"Name's Starbuck. Not nothing to do with them."

Flood's mouth gaped. "Starbuck? Ain't you the one we hired to look after Orville—the man the marshal recommended to us?"

Shawn nodded.

"And now instead you show up here with a ransom note for fifty thousand dollars—what the hell kind of a deal are you working? You giving us a double-cross or something?"

Starbuck shook his head. "Little hard to explain. We've had trouble from the start. Twice the same man tried to get to your brother, kill him. Then night before last a different bunch got into his room at a hotel, kidnapped them and—"

"Where the devil were you?"

"Across the hall. Two lawmen and myself stood guard but—"

"But you let them get to Orville and my niece just the same? If that's what you call protecting—"

"A man died there that night protecting them—the sheriff of Bonnerville," Starbuck said coldly. "I figure I'm due some blame for what's happened but I won't hear of you or anybody else running down the men who gave me a hand. They took it on themselves as a favor to me. . . . What about the ransom—you paying it?"

Flood brushed angrily at his mustache. "Got no choice! Too much time and money invested in Orville to dump him—that goddamn Lester knows that."

"You acquainted with him?"

"Plenty. Used to work for me—right here in this office. Expect that's when he got the idea to pull this, and you can tell him when you get back that I'm not letting him get away with it—not by a damn sight!"

Starbuck shrugged. "Way it stands now, you or nobody else can tell him much of anything. He and that bunch he's got with him would as soon kill your brother and your niece as draw a breath. Going to have to walk easy until they're safe."

"I can get you all the help you want—men to ride in a posse, maybe even some soldiers. Happens I know the commanding officer at the fort pretty well—"

"The last thing you want to try. Lester's got two of his bunch riding herd on me. Watch every move I make. If I leave here with some help, or you put a posse to following me, you're the same as signing a death warrant for your brother and Carla."

"But—fifty thousand dollars! I—we—can't just let them get away with it."

"You've got no choice except to pay off—at least right now. Then, after your brother and his daughter are safe, you can move in, do what you please to get your money back."

"Be a little late then," Flood mused, and suddenly fixed his hard stare on Shawn. "Just occurred to me—I'll be trusting all that money to you. What's to keep you from heading in the other direction, double-crossing all of us?"

"Nothing, I reckon," Starbuck replied coldly. "Only I don't figure to."

"All I've got's your word—"

"That's all."

"Guess I've got no choice," Flood said with a sigh. "It's going to take a little time to get that much money together."

"You'll have to make it fast. Lester gave me until Thursday at sundown to be back there with it."

"I know—says that there in the letter." Flood reached for his hat—a dark, narrow-brimmed beaver—and placed it on his head. "Where'll you be?"

"Intend to drop by the marshal's office, let him know what's going on—"

"Forget it. He's up Taos way. Something about

a shooting. I'll tell him when he gets back."

Starbuck grinned wryly. He could guess what Flood would say to the lawman where he was concerned. "I'll be at Valdez's livery stable. When can I expect you?"

"Let's set it for six o'clock. That ought to give me enough time."

Starbuck nodded, turned for the door, and left the building. He returned to the plaza, and seeking out a restaurant, sat down at a table and ordered a meal. He took little enjoyment from it, however, his mind being filled with a growing worry for Orville and Carla Flood.

He had been too engrossed in making the ride to Santa Fe and in getting in touch with Carl Flood to give their position much thought earlier, but now that the arrangements had been made, he had time to reflect. Orville, of course, would be all right as long as he kept to himself and didn't antagonize the outlaws, but Carla was a different matter.

She was a beautiful girl, and despite Cole Lester's assurance, she was in great danger. Her sharp tongue was no protection from the outlaws, who, with time hanging heavy on their hands, could find her far too attractive to resist. And Orville Flood would be powerless to help her. He could only hope that his warning to Lester and the others would carry some weight.

But even if the outlaws lived up to Cole

Lester's word where the girl was concerned, there would come that time after the money was handed over and the outlaws had no further use for the Floods or him. Starbuck had no illusions as to what could happen then, for Lester and the others, wanting no witnesses left behind, would take immediate steps to avoid such.

It wasn't going to be as easy for them as they might suspect, Starbuck decided, finishing his meal with a final cup of coffee. He wasn't about to give in without a fight.

Leaving the restaurant, he sauntered down the street, making himself easily visible to Mendoza or Frick, whichever one was keeping tabs on him. Coming to a saloon, he paused in front for a few moments and then stepped inside.

Nodding to the bartender, he continued on through the low-ceilinged, shadow-filled building, exited by the rear door, and doubled back up to a gun shop he had noted earlier. There he purchased a five shot, forty-one caliber pistol of the hideaway type popular with gamblers, and a dozen rounds of ammunition. After testing the weapon's action, he thrust it inside his shirt, anchoring it under his belt, and retraced his steps to the saloon.

Treating himself to a drink of rye whiskey, Shawn returned to the street and made his way leisurely to the livery barn where he had stabled the sorrel. He was feeling better for the bit of strategy he had come up with; now, when he returned to the outlaws and Lester relieved him of his holstered gun, he would still have the forty-one to fall back on.

Shortly before six o'clock the hostler roused him from the pile of hay where he was napping. Following the man up the runway to the office, he found Carl Flood awaiting him.

"Saddle my horse," Shawn said to the stableman, and when he had gone, turned to face Flood. He pointed to a leather satchel the man was holding. "That it?"

Flood nodded. "Fifty thousand in currency and gold. That's the way Lester wanted it."

Starbuck reached for the bag, hesitated as Flood passed it to him, but maintained a grip on the handle.

"Expect you to get to the law fast as you can after you turn this over to Lester," the older man said. "I want a posse combing the country no more'n an hour after you do that. And something else—I'll be expecting you to furnish me with the names and descriptions of the rest of Lester's gang. We're not throwing away fifty thousand dollars!"

Shawn pulled the satchel free of Carl Flood's grasp, tucked it under his arm as inconspicuously as possible. Frowning, he ducked his head toward the hostler, now leading the saddled and bridled sorrel up the runway to them.

Flood ignored the cautioning. "You hear me?" he demanded.

Shawn, taut with anger, dug into his pocket for a silver dollar, flipped it to the stableman, and swung onto the saddle. Leaning down, he faced the politician.

"I heard you," he said with a tight smile. "I'm just hoping he didn't . . . Far as your list goes, you'll get it, assuming I'm alive to make one."

Raking the sorrel with his spurs, he rode past the man and out into the fading sunlight.

12

The gelding had benefitted noticeably from the feeding and few hours rest, but he was still far from in peak condition. It would have been better to wait until morning before starting the return trip, Starbuck realized, thus allowing the horse to enjoy a full night's rest, but his worry for Carla Flood would not permit it. The sooner he placed the money in Cole Lester's hands, the sooner the girl would be out of danger.

He trusted Carl Flood not at all, and from time to time he glanced back over his shoulder for indications that he was being followed—not that he expected the man to make an effort to recover the money, but he did fear the possibility of Flood taking matters into his own hands, despite the warning given, and dispatching soldiers or a party of armed riders to trail him in the hope of capturing Cole Lester and the others.

But as the miles wore on and he neither saw nor heard sounds of pursuit, he dismissed the thought from his mind. He took the same route as he had come, mostly because it was the shortest and not because he wanted to make it easy for Frick and Mendoza. There was no need to consider them; Lester had worked everything out carefully and he knew the two outlaws would be on hand when the proper moment came.

Around midnight he halted to rest the gelding. Finding a bit of coffee in his saddlebags and using the small lard tin he carried for such purpose, he built a fire and boiled up a helping of strong, bitter brew. He drank it from the tin, searing his throat a bit as he did, but it jarred him into wakefulness and washed away some of the weariness that dragged at his body despite the several hours sleep he had gotten.

Again in the saddle, he tried to work up a practical plan for those first moments when he rejoined the outlaws and the showdown was upon him. But there was little he could do; the actions of Cole Lester and the others would dictate his movements. It would simply be up to him to take advantage of even the smallest opportunity to get the Floods and himself to safety.

Again he began to doze, head slumped forward, chin sunk into his chest. He shook himself, rubbed at his eyes vigorously, fought to stay awake. The sorrel just might take a wrong turn, and while he was certain Mendoza and Frick were somewhere in the offing, he didn't want to sacrifice any time by—

"Pull up!"

The sharp command brought Starbuck upright in the saddle. The gelding stopped of his own accord and Shawn, suddenly tense, strained to see ahead in the weak light of the early morning hour. He was in a small clearing. A tall man wearing a yellow slicker that reached to his spurs, a mask across his face and a hat pulled low on his head, blocked the trail.

"Climb down!"

Shawn, thoroughly awake, tried to recognize the voice. His first thought was that it was one of the outlaws out to cheat his partners and claim all of the ransom money for himself, but it didn't sound like any of them. Certainly it was not Mendoza or Lonnie Frick. And it wasn't Lester—there was no similarity in the vaguely familiar voice. The man was too tall for Ed Jacks.

"You hear? Get off that horse!"

Starbuck came off the gelding slowly, making no unnecessary moves. Through the hush he heard a horse off somewhere in the deep shadows stamp restlessly. Evidently the holdup man had been waiting for some time.

"Get your hands up—high!"

The outlaw moved the pistol he was holding at full cock suggestively, the very motion indicating that he was not in the least averse to using it.

Shawn lifted his arms. "What the hell's this all about?"

"Fifty thousand dollars," the masked man drawled. "Reckon that's it there in that satchel."

Surprise rocked Starbuck. How could he, if he was not Lester or one of the kidnapping gang, know of the ransom money—the exact amount?

His thoughts flipped back to Santa Fe, to the runway of the stable where he had met with Carl Flood; had someone overheard, perhaps witnessed the transfer of the money—ridden ahead and laid an ambush? It seemed hardly possible.

Stalling, raking his mind for a logical explanation, and a way out, Shawn shrugged. "You're loco, mister. Where'd I get that kind of money?"

"From a man named Flood—in Santa Fe," the robber snapped. "Don't think you can fool an old fooler—I know that's it there in that satchel! Now unhook it, toss it over here—easy like."

There had to be some connection with Santa Fe; either the hijacker had overheard Flood talking in the livery stable or else had known about the ransom earlier, possibly gotten wind of it while the politician was getting the money together. It was the only explanation.

Starbuck shook his head. "You'll have to come get it—I won't hand it over. Happens it's too important for me to do that. If I don't get it delivered, there're two people—"

"The hell with them," the outlaw cut in. "I'm looking out for myself. Get it."

Shawn did not move. The most welcome sight he could think of at that moment would be Cruz Mendoza and Lonnie Frick, but either they had lost him in the darkness or they were not keeping as close a watch over him as Cole Lester expected.

"You doing what I tell you or am I going to have to use my iron?"

"I don't figure you will," Starbuck replied, "else you would've shot me out of the saddle, not bothered to just stop me."

"That's where you're wrong. For fifty thousand I'd do anything. Only reason I haven't put a bullet in you is I don't want somebody hearing a gunshot."

Then the vaquero and Frick *were* in the area and the holdup man was aware of it! Or could it be the posse from Bonnerville still prowling the countryside in search of him?

"The bag—throw it over here or, by God, I'll drop you right where you're standing!"

Shawn delayed, pushing his luck—for just what, he did not really know. Off in the fading darkness a night bird called softly, and a faint breeze coming in with the approaching dawn rustled the leaves.

"I ain't waiting no longer!" the masked man snarled, and raised the weapon in his hand chesthigh.

Shawn stared at the round, black hole at the end of the weapon's barrel and shrugged. He'd gone as far as he dared, but gained nothing. All there was left to do now was surrender the money, hope he could later track down the outlaw and recover it.

He started to pivot, reach for the satchel

attached to his saddle by several rawhide strings. A quiet rustling in the brush checked him, and from the corner of his eye he saw the holdup man look back in alarm.

Starbuck reacted instantly. His hand swept down for the gun on his hip—and in the next fragment of time the clearing seemed to explode in his face as a wave of blackness engulfed him.

13

Starbuck rose slowly to consciousness. He lay quiet, biding his time, instinct holding him motionless until he was certain he was alone. When that became apparent he sat up. His head throbbed with a relentless force and there was a stinging along his left ear.

He raised a hand, gingerly explored the affected area. His fingers encountered a damp stickiness, and he realized the side of his face was covered with blood. The burning came from the ear. The meaning of it all came to him; a bullet had grazed his head, clipped off a bit of skin in its passage. The wound was slight but had bled freely.

Dazed, he looked around. It was much lighter now and he could see no sign of the bushwhacker—or of the sorrel. He swore deeply at that. He was miles from anywhere—afoot; Santa Fe lay many hours of steady riding to the east, Bonnerville was somewhere to the south—or would it be the west? It was difficult to think clearly.

He pulled himself to his feet, staggering a bit in the effort. Pain rolled through him in a fresh rush and needles of light stabbed at his eyes, but he held himself upright, fought off the swirling sickness with its accompanying weakness.

After a few moments the nausea passed and he began to move about falteringly. It seemed to help. His brain cleared, started to function more normally. Halting, he studied the ground before him. The sorrel must be close by; the outlaw, believing him dead, would not have burdened himself with an extra horse for which he had no need. Such would only hinder his flight. The masked man was intent on but one thing—getting the fifty thousand dollars and leaving the country as fast as he could.

With the rim of the sun breaking over the horizon to the east, Shawn began to search about for hoof prints, wondering what it was that had distracted the outlaw momentarily. Some small animal, perhaps, or it could have been another rider—a member of the posse, or maybe Mendoza or Frick. Whichever, he had almost been afforded his chance for escape—but only almost; instead it had resulted in his missing death by only a fraction.

Shortly he came upon the tracks he sought, followed them for a brief distance, halted, relief filling him. The sorrel was standing in a small patch of open ground a dozen yards farther on, grazing quietly on the thin grass. The gunshot had spooked him, sent him plunging off into the brush.

Starbuck crossed hurriedly to the waiting horse. There was the chance the outlaw had not been able to catch the gelding, get the saddle. The money could still be safe. . . . It was wishful thinking, Shawn knew, but he held to the faint hope until he reached the gelding, saw the leather strings hanging loose. In his haste the thief had not bothered to loosen the knots, had slashed the thongs with his knife.

Shrugging, Starbuck took his canteen, helped himself to a swallow, and then, soaking his neckerchief, bathed the wound on the side of his head and cleaned his face. He began to feel better after that, and returning the container of water to its place, he began to search about for the tracks of the holdup man's horse. If he could locate them, overtake the outlaw, and recover the money, there was still room to meet Cole Lester's deadline.

His thoughts came to a sudden halt. Somewhere close to his right he heard the sound of a walking horse—of several horses. He stepped hurriedly to the sorrel, led him deep into the brush.

"How much farther we going?" an impatient voice called.

"How the hell do I know!" The reply was ragged, heavy with disgust. "Jimson's running this thing, not me. Ask him."

The posse . . . Shawn smiled grimly. They were still looking for him—and their presence likely accounted for the absence of Mendoza and Lonnie Frick.

"Hey, Jimson!" It was the first voice again.

"Yeah, Will?"

"Ain't it about time to call it quits? I'm—"

"You heard that gunshot," Jimson answered. "Came from around here, somewheres close. We ain't pulling out till we know who fired it."

"Well, there ain't nobody around here now. Whoever done it's gone for sure."

"Could be you're right, but it's hard to tell about a gunshot. Let's pull up. I'll call in the rest of the boys."

A pistol cracked, the report echoing flatly through the early morning. One of the men swore.

"That was a fool stunt! If that Starbuck's around he'll hightail it now for certain—fast as he can go."

"How else was I going to hail the others in?" Jimson said in a weary tone. "Was the signal we agreed on."

Well-hidden in the brush, Shawn listened to the constant bickering. Evidently the posse had not made a return trip to Bonnerville for the night, had instead kept up a search for him. All of the men were worn and nerves were sharp. He gave brief thought to showing himself to the party, laying his situation before them, then brushed it aside. In their present mood they would believe nothing he said and he could only put himself in a worse position.

Jimson's deep voice reached him. "We ain't getting nowheres. All we've done is rub saddle sores on our tails chasing around like we've been. I figured we'd be better off to head back toward Blackman Mountain. We know for sure he was headed that way."

"Was yesterday—or the day before—or whenever it was. I plumb lost track of time. . . . Anyways, I'm betting he's clean out of the country."

"Same here . . . I don't think there's no use going back to the mountain. Hell, we've worked out them hollers and flats and arroyos a half-dozen times!"

There was silence following that, broken shortly by the creak of leather and the slow thump of horses' hooves as other riders joined the meeting.

After a bit someone said, "Jimson figures we ought to go back to Blackman Mountain."

A mixed response greeted that. The man called Will said, "I don't see much sense doing anything but heading for home. We been out here trying—"

"We're going to keep on looking," Jimson cut in sharply. "We let a killer get away scot free and a big man get kidnapped, along with his daughter. Up to us to bring him and the rest of his bunch in."

"If he done it—"

"What do you mean if he done it? Ernie Quinn surprised him hunkered over Bert's body, didn't he? Said he thought he'd seen a knife in his hand. Then this here Starbuck took off like a turpentined cat. What more proof you needing, Asa?"

"Now, that ain't real proof, Earl—"

"Is to me!"

"Well, proof or not," Jimson said in a gusty voice, "we got to catch him and them others before we can do anything. . . . Anybody seen Jess Carr? Him being the deputy, it ought to be him here saying what's to be done."

"Run into him a ways back. Was about midnight. He'll be showing up pretty soon, I reckon."

"Probably doing his scouting over around the mountain," Jimson said. "Let's be heading back that way. Now, watch sharp. It being daylight, this job's going to be a whole lot easier."

Shawn listened to the sounds of the men mounting, the receding tunk-a-tunk sound of their horses as they moved off. He had been right about Quinn and the gathering in front of the jail; the clerk had been accusing him of the sheriff's murder. He hadn't given it much thought then but now it angered him. After a moment he shrugged. He'd iron it all out later, somehow. Right now he needed to get on the trail of the man who'd taken the ransom money.

Looping the sorrel's reins about a clump of oak,

he walked back to where he had been standing when the outlaw's bullet grazed him. From that point he figured out the spot where the man had been standing, crossed to it. There were several well-embedded heel marks. Backtracking from there, he located the place in the brush where the robber had picketed his horse. After that it was a simple task to find the trail of the man as he had ridden off—due south.

Grimly satisfied, Starbuck returned to the sorrel, freed the reins, and went onto the saddle. The outlaw had a considerable start on him but the tracks he was leaving behind were plain. It wouldn't take long to overtake him.

14

The outlaw continued to bear south. Shawn, eyes reaching ahead of the loping sorrel, followed the prints with little difficulty. As long as the rider held to the edge of the brush along which he was making his way it was a simple matter to follow.

But near mid-morning the long ribbon of ragged growth petered out and the flat he was crossing rose gradually to a rough, flinty plateau. The hoof marks were no longer quickly seen and he was compelled to slow, proceed with more care.

He did not lose the trail altogether. For a short distance he might find no trace of the passing horse, then farther on he would locate a clearly defined track and so would press on. But it was turning into a time-consuming chore. Several times Shawn cast a worried glance at the sun, well on its mid-point course in the arching sky; at the rate he was traveling he could chase the outlaw for a week and not catch up, he decided bitterly.

He had no choice, however, but to continue. Enlisting the aid of the posse was out of the question, and returning to the area where he could again get in contact with Cole Lester through Mendoza and Frick, who had apparently lost him entirely, would be useless. The kidnappers were interested only in his delivering the money to them on time in order that they could make good an escape.

He could do nothing but go on. It was only common sense to believe the outlaw ahead would be forced to stop some time, even if for only a few minutes. No horse could travel constantly without rest.

Noon passed and the long, hot afternoon hours began. The sorrel began to show signs of tiring, of needing water, but Starbuck kept after him. He would have to stop soon, he knew, but he would hold off as long as possible. Reaching up, he caught the brim of his hat, carefully settled it lower on his head to cut down the glare from the glistening sand and the mirroring slabs of rock. Overhead the sky was a cloudless, burnished bowl across which a few birds made their way. To all intents and purposes, he was a solitary pilgrim in a vast world.

Abruptly he pulled the gelding to a halt. He had lost the trail. Leaning forward in the saddle, he scanned the ground ahead of him. It was rough, hard-baked, and studded with rock. Wheeling about, he backtracked a short distance, picked up the hoof prints; he was going right, he saw. The outlaw had not swung off, had continued up the grade. The soil was simply too hard-surfaced to record the marks.

Relieved, Shawn urged the sorrel onto the crest of the rise. It appeared to be some sort of vantage point, and, with luck, he might be able to get a glimpse of the man he was following in the distance. He reached the lip of the butte, drew up in surprise. Below him lay Bonnerville.

Starbuck stared at the scatter of buildings, the gray-green of trees and shrubbery. Unfamiliar with the country, he had not realized the course he was following would lead him back to the settlement. He had thought the town to be farther west—but there it lay, silent and dusty in the late afternoon sunlight.

And the now visible prints of the outlaw's horse led down the slope to it.

Starbuck considered that thoughtfully. The town was no safe place for him. Although many of the townsmen would still be out in the posse that was scouring the country for him, there would still be plenty of others who would recognize him and react instantly.

It would be smart to hold off until dark, then ride in, but the urgency pressing him brushed such discretion aside. He had to get that money, hurry it to Cole Lester—and the man that had it was somewhere in the settlement. There was but one good possibility; if he could locate Frank Ogden he could get help from him.

But first he should do all possible to change his appearance. Removing his hat, he crushed it into a compact mass and thrust it into one of his saddlebags. Digging into the other, he procured a faded green brush jacket, pulled it on. This altered his looks slightly, and anyone glancing at him casually might pass him by. The big gelding, however, was a different matter. There was no disguising his size and his bright red coat. He could only hope that there had been just a few who noticed him upon their arrival in the town.

Moving on, he resumed the trail of the outlaw, definite again in the soft sand, and descended the grade. The prints led him around the first of the houses, across the main street a hundred yards or so north of the business district, and swung in finally to the rear of the buildings.

Looking beyond, watchful for anyone moving about, Starbuck saw a livery barn set back a distance from the structures, and following the line of tracks, bore toward it. It was not the one in which he'd stabled the gelding, which lessened the problem somewhat since he would not be encountering the same hostler.

Guiding the horse to a corral that extended off one side of the building, Shawn pulled up. A trough of water brought the sorrel's ears forward anxiously and Starbuck led him through the open gate, waited a long minute while the animal eased his thirst. That done with, he looped the reins about a nearby snubbing post.

Tension was building within him as he crossed

the littered yard and quietly entered the shadowy depths of the stable. Halting just within the doorway, he permitted his eyes to adjust to the change of light, and then, hand riding the butt of his pistol, he moved on.

The first two stalls were empty; a chunky little pinto gelding occupied the third. Starbuck slipped in beside the horse, laid a palm against its flank. It was warm, sweaty. The hair on the animal's back where the saddle had ridden was still matted flat.

Taut, Starbuck stepped again into the runway. There were two more horses farther on; he examined both, found them cold. Undoubtedly they had not seen use that day. Wheeling, Shawn turned to the hostler's office at the front of the stable. An elderly man in dirty, torn overalls and undershirt was standing in the doorway eyeing him suspiciously.

"You looking for something?"

Starbuck pointed to the pinto. "That horse—when did he come in?"

"Couple hours ago."

That tallied. "Who does he belong to?"

The hostler spat, cocked his head to one side. "You're asking a mighty lot of questions, mister. . . . I ain't sure it's any of your business who—"

Temper flared through Starbuck. He had no time to waste bandying words. His hand shot forward, caught the stableman by the bib of his overalls.

"Answer me!" he snarled, jerking the man into the runway. "Who rode that horse in?"

The hostler's eyes widened. He swallowed noisily, tried to pull away.

"Now, there ain't no use getting mean—"

"Who?" Shawn demanded, shaking the man roughly.

"Jess Carr, the deputy sheriff."

15

Jess Carr! Starbuck stared unseeingly at the old man. It was hard to believe, but there could be no mistake. He had trailed the highjacker in from the point of the holdup, and as further proof, there was the horse that had been used, still sweaty.

Releasing his grasp on the hostler, Shawn stepped back. New thoughts were crowding into his mind, along with questions that seemed to instantly find their own answers. Did Carr have a connection with Cole Lester and his bunch? Was he working with them, actually one of the gang? Was he the one who had made possible the kidnapping of the Floods—at the expense of Bert Wilger's life? Being one of the town's lawmen, it would have been easy for him to move about, set up the arrangements.

There were no answers other than yes; otherwise, how would Carr have known about the ransom, of where it came from, and its exact amount? How else would he know where to wait in ambush to hijack the money—something further simplified for him by the presence of the posse he presumably was leading, since its movements kept Mendoza and Lonnie Frick out of the general area. . . . But double-crossing his outlaw partners would be a dangerous game, one wherein success depended upon there being no witness to the hijacking.

"Where's the deputy now?"

The stableman shrugged. "How'd I know?" he asked peevishly. "Down at the jail, I reckon."

Shawn pivoted, started to retrace his steps to the sorrel, paused. Reaching into a pocket he produced a silver dollar, flipped it to the man.

"Keep your mouth shut about me, savvy?"

The hostler deftly caught the coin, nodded, but his eyes had narrowed and a half smile pulled at his lips.

"You never saw me—remember that," Starbuck said, and continued on.

He walked the length of the runway, stepped out into the corral, and crossed to the waiting sorrel. The sun was now dropping low and the late afternoon coolness was beginning to set in. There would soon be more people on the street.

He considered the wisdom of waiting until full dark before going after Carr, decided that if he was careful, the risk would not be too great. He was reluctant to lose even an hour; the lives of Carla and Orville Flood depended on his recovering the money and getting it to Cole Lester before the stated deadline, drawing steadily nearer—and just how much of a problem he would encounter in gaining possession of the ransom he had no way of knowing.

Going to the saddle, he rode out of the corral. The most logical place to find Carr, as the hostler had said, was at the jail. Shawn recalled the alleyway behind it, and the rear door to the building. The likelihood of not being seen by anyone would be greater there. Accordingly, he turned the sorrel into that direction.

Shortly he slowed the gelding's pace. He was approaching one of the cross streets. On the opposite side he saw the beginning of the alley down which he wished to travel. Once he crossed over he would be comparatively safe, but reaching it would be risky as he was now near the center of the town. But it was a gamble he had to take, and lowering his head, he rode into the open.

Instantly a shout went up. Shawn swung his attention to the left, toward the sound. A dozen horsemen had pulled up in the intersection not ten yards distant and were staring at him. He had blundered into the returning posse.

"It's him!" a voice yelled in surprise.

Starbuck threw himself forward on the gelding, started to wheel, hoping to make a run for it back the way he had come. Guns barked spitefully. Dust kicked up around the sorrel.

"Don't try it!" one of the riders warned.

Muttering an oath, Shawn settled back on the saddle. There would be no outrunning a hail of bullets from the guns leveled at him. He raised his hands slowly as the posse members closed in about him.

"Wouldn't you know it!" the familiar voice of the man called Will lamented. "All the time we was out there beating the brush, he was right here in town!"

Starbuck felt a hand at his hip, a lightness as someone lifted his pistol from its holster. A voice close by spoke.

"What'll we do with him, Jimson?"

The apparent leader of the posse, a big, hulking man on a chunky buckskin, kneed his mount in to where he faced Shawn. His skin was an angry red from the sun and wind, and his deep-set eyes were bloodshot.

"Know what we ought to do," he said in a low, grating tone. "String him up, that's what—the goddamn murdering—"

"You're way off," Starbuck cut in coldly. "Wilger was dead when I found him."

"Not how Ernie Quinn tells it."

"Quinn's a liar!"

"Sure he is! And I reckon you ain't got nothing to do with the kidnapping of Orville Flood and his daughter, either! You want to tell us now where you got them hid out?"

It could be a mistake to bring the posse in on the kidnapping. Chances were good they would go charging off into the Blackman Trail country in search of Lester and his prisoners, and bring about the death of the Floods.

"I don't know where they are," Starbuck said, truthfully. "And I'm not hiding them out. Kidnapping was done by a gang of outlaws. I've been trying to get them turned loose. Rode to San—"

"You must think we're mighty dumb around here," Jimson said. "We ain't, even if this is a little town. We know you and your bunch set up this kidnapping and then pulled it off here, figuring you could easy get away with it. Bert Wilger found out what was going on so you killed him. Now, ain't that the how of it?"

Starbuck stirred wearily. "You're about as far from the truth as you can get. I was hired by the men backing Flood to look out for him. I'm still doing that—"

"Yeah, you sure are!" one of the riders said with a laugh.

Bystanders, attracted by the group of riders halted in the middle of the street, were beginning to gather, ask their questions. Shawn scanned them hopefully in search of Frank Ogden. The driver was not to be seen. He shifted impatiently on the saddle. Time was slipping by.

"One way I can straighten this all out," he said, directing the words to Jimson. "Take me to Carr."

"He ain't in town," a rider volunteered. "Last we seen of him he was back in the hills—hunting you and your bunch."

"He's here. Trailed him in myself."

Jimson frowned, rubbed at the stubble on his chin. "Reckon he must've rode in ahead of us. . . . Why you wanting to see him? What's he got to do with it?"

"Everything," Starbuck said flatly. "Let's find him."

Jimson glanced over the posse and the growing crowd, then grinned and bobbed his head. "Well, I reckon that won't be no big chore, seeing as how we're taking you to jail anyway, and that's where Jess'll be if he's here."

Starbuck made no comment as he swung the sorrel about and moved off up the street, the posse members surrounding him in a tight circle. He wasn't certain just how he should handle Jess Carr; the frame of mind Jimson and the other men were in was such that he knew they would believe only what the deputy would say, and scoff at any accusations he'd make. But he had to start somewhere; he was accomplishing nothing there in the street except the loss of time.

Odgen. . . . The question of the old driver's whereabouts again posed itself. Shawn turned to the rider nearest him, started to ask, and then let the words die. If Frank was in a jail cell, also suspected of being in on the kidnapping and murder, he'd know it soon enough; if not, that meant he was still free and a potential source of help.

16

Pocketed among the posse members, Starbuck rode silently toward Bonnerville's main street. They reached the corner, then angled right. The crowd that had gathered earlier was clustered around them. Immediately people moving idly along the sidewalks paused to stare.

"They got him!" a man shouted abruptly as recognition came to him. "They got that killer!"

Others took up the cry. The crowd began to increase. The procession slowed, came almost to a halt as the street before it filled. Jimson, worried lines appearing on his haggard features, glanced at the men to his left and right.

"Tip—Rufus, you two give me a hand here," he said, and pushed out ahead of the other riders a stride or so. "Crowd's getting ugly."

The three men lined up abreast, forming a blunt wedge. The people directly in front of them began to fall back. From somewhere in their midst a voice shouted.

"Why'd you bring him in? Why didn't you string him up when you caught him?"

Jimson drew his pistol, fired a shot into the air. The yells subsided. "Just keep on moving," he said over his shoulder, and then turned back to the crowd.

"Maybe we had the notion," he continued, shouting to make himself heard. "Bert Wilger was maybe my best friend, only we ain't doing something like that around here. This is a good town and there ain't going to be no lynching on its conscience."

"Then what're you going to do with him?"

"Putting him in the lock-up—letting the law deal with him."

"The law'll hang him," the man called Tip added. "You can bank on that."

Starbuck, tense, looked ahead. They were almost to the jail. Although lamps had been lit in many shops along the way, it was still dark inside the low, squat building.

"Where the hell's that deputy?" Jimson muttered, giving the place a critical glance. "Ought've showed himself before now if he's around."

"He ain't," Tip said as they pulled up to the hitchrack and drew aside to let Starbuck's horse through. "Can bet on that."

Jimson swore feelingly. "Well, get in there and light some lamps," he said, and again faced the crowd, now fanning out in front of the structure.

"Telling you all to stay back, hear? Don't want none of you getting hurt."

There were a few scattered replies. Jimson swung off his saddle, motioned to Shawn, who, pausing long enough to reclaim his hat, followed.

The remainder of the posse began to dismount, shuffle wearily over to the front of the building and take up positions there. Inside Tip had got the lamps going.

"Keep moving," Jimson said in a low voice to Shawn. "We been plenty lucky so far. Best we don't push it."

Starbuck crossed the landing, stepped up into the small office. Tip and Rufus caught him by the arms at once, propelled him toward the cells that stood off a short hallway at the rear. Behind him he heard Jimson yell to the crowd: "You folks might as well go on home. Show's over." Then he closed the door.

There were no occupants in either of the two cells, Starbuck saw with relief as the men with him drew to a halt before them. Ogden had managed to avoid arrest—assuming the townspeople believed him to also be involved in the kidnapping and murder. Frank could possibly come to his aid if he was still around, but Starbuck knew he could not depend on it, must instead rely on his own resources.

He still had his one ace in the hole—the hideaway pistol he'd purchased in Santa Fe for use when he met with Lester and the other outlaws. He would watch his chances, bring it into play when the time was right—necessarily when he had fewer men to deal with.

Rufus rattled the doors of the barred cubicles,

swore impatiently. "You see the key in there somewheres, Jimson? Damned cells are locked."

A moment later the posse leader said, "Ain't hanging on the peg—and I don't see it nowheres else. The deputy must have it on him."

Rufus cursed again, turned Shawn about, and pushed him back into the office. "Means we're going to have to set here and wait."

Tip seized the back of the swivel chair at the desk, spun it about, and sent it rolling up against a back wall. He motioned to Starbuck.

"Get over there and set down."

Jimson crossed to the door as Shawn settled into the chair. "You two stay put, I'm going out and find Carr," he said, and stepped out into the night.

Rufus sighed, sank onto one of the benches opposite Starbuck. Tip, taking out his sack of tobacco and fold of brown papers, sat down beside him.

"I'm hoping Jimson finds him pretty quick," he said wearily. "I'm plumb beat."

"Amen," Rufus murmured.

Starbuck watched the rider roll his smoke, but his thoughts were on Jess Carr. It was conceivable Jimson would not find him, he was realizing with growing apprehension. The deputy, fearing reprisal from Cole Lester and the rest of his outlaw friends, could have deemed it wise to get out of the country as fast as possible—hopefully before his partners even became aware that he had hijacked the ransom money. It would be the logical course for him to follow.

Abruptly the door opened. Rufus and Tip came to their feet, guns in hand. It was one of the posse members.

"Goddammit, Ike—you know better'n to come busting in here like that!" Tip said, resuming his seat.

"Could've got yourself shot," Rufus added. "What's up?"

"Nothing," Ike replied, his face reddening with embarrassment. "Only wanted to say things've settled down. Crowd's gone—same as the rest of the boys. Jimson wanted me to tell you he'd send somebody to spell you if he don't find that deputy pretty quick."

"You see him, tell him to make it soon," Tip said heavily.

Ike nodded, withdrew. Tip began to roll himself another cigarette after offering the makings to Rufus, who refused. Shawn faced them from across the room. The odds were much better for an escape now that the posse members outside had moved on and the crowd in the street had dispersed, but his chances of making a clean break were still slim.

Both Tip and Rufus had their weapons out and in their laps, ready for instant use. He might stop one with the hideaway gun but he knew he would never get off a second shot should they take it in mind to stop him.

An appearance by Jess Carr would help matters some, although he would prefer to escape, hunt the lawman down himself; in the long run such would save much time since Carr, when he showed up at the jail, would put him in a cell immediately, all the while laughing off accusations and claiming them to be the desperate words of a man trying to save himself from the gallows. Once alone with the deputy he could make use of the hideaway gun, but many hours would be lost probably.

And all could be lost if Carr had already taken flight.

Starbuck considered that grimly as the conviction that such had occurred grew stronger. He couldn't afford to just sit and wait. He must act. Turning his head he glanced through the barred window that faced the street. He could see no one, but there could be loiterers near the building who were not visible to him.

Somewhere down the way a man yelled at a passing rider, the drumming of the horse's hooves sounding faint and hollow inside the stuffy room. Rufus yawned loudly, rubbed at his jaw.

"Sure do wish somebody'd show up," he mumbled.

Shawn's eyes hesitated briefly on the man, moved on as he continued to search for an idea, a thought—anything that would permit him to escape. His gaze halted on the water bucket and the tin dipper hooked to its rim. A plan quickly took shape in his mind—desperate but possible. He stirred, pulled himself upright in the chair.

"All right if I get myself a drink of water?" he asked, pointing at the bucket.

Tip glared at him morosely, glanced at Rufus who seemed to be dozing. After a moment he nodded. "Get it—but don't try nothing."

Shawn rose to his feet, crossed to the table upon which the galvanized container had been placed. The plan was simple. He would have his back to the men. With the dipper in his right hand, he would draw the hideaway pistol with the right. While Tip and Rufus were thus off guard, he would spin, hurl the dipper full of water at one, level the gun, and fire, if necessary, at the other.

With a little luck he wouldn't have to trigger his weapon but would be able to disarm the pair without facing the consequences that a gunshot was sure to bring. The sorrel was at the hitchrack in front. Once he had knocked out the two posse members, he'd slip through the doorway, mount the gelding, and make for the nearest cover. Darkness would make escape, once he was outside the building, fairly simple.

Then he would be free to hunt down Jess Carr, recover the ransom money, and by hard riding, make the connection with Lester and the outlaws before the deadline. And if Carr had disappeared, taking the money with him? Starbuck gave that thought; he'd search for Carr as long as possible, and if he failed to find him, return to Cole Lester and explain what had happened. Maybe he'd be able to make the outlaw see reason.

"Come on, come on! Don't be lollygagging there all night."

It was Tip's voice, ragged and impatient. Shawn, holding the dipper to his lips, turned his head, paused at his drinking.

"Pretty dry. Last water I had was early this morning."

Tip muttered a reply as he again faced the bucket. With the container still at his mouth, he slid his right hand inside his shirt. Wrapping his fingers around the butt of the pistol, he worked it back until it nestled in his palm and he had a thumb hooked over the hammer, a forefinger on the trigger. Bending slightly, he refilled the dipper.

He would throw it at Tip. Rufus, half asleep, would be the lesser problem. He should be able to overcome both men without firing a shot.

"All right, you've had enough. Get yourself back—"

Tip's irritated voice broke off. Starbuck, at the point of pivoting, dipper of water and pistol ready for use, froze. The door of the jail swung inward. Relief stirred through Shawn. It was Jess Carr.

17

Surprise blanked the deputy's features. Starbuck suppressed a smile. Carr had thought for an instant that he was seeing a ghost and the shock had been like a blow.

Tip lowered his pistol, holstered it. "Where the hell you been?" he demanded sourly.

Rufus, fully awake and on his feet, started at once for the door. "He's all your'n," he said. "You see Jimson?"

Jess Carr, astonishment still evident in his eyes, shook his head. "Just rode in. Got my horse out back—ain't even took time to stable him."

Shawn considered the lawman coolly. There was no truth in that statement, he knew, and if there was a horse waiting out behind the jail it was there for but one purpose; Carr was planning to leave town. Likely he had dropped by the jail to pick up something of his.

Tip moved to follow his partner, frowned. "This bird claims you was here already—"

"Not me," Carr said briskly, stepping into the office. "Got his lines mixed up." He had fully recovered himself. "Sure do owe you gents a lot for bringing him in. Would've been out there yet myself if it hadn't got dark."

"Hell, he was right here in town all the time,"

Rufus said, his voice filled with disgust. "Weren't no use of none of us being out there pounding leather."

"Why ain't he locked up?"

"Couldn't find the key," Tip replied promptly. "We figured you had it on you."

Carr turned to the gun rack at one end of the room, reached inside it, and produced the ring of heavy keys.

"Right here all the time," he said. "Was too handy there on the peg. Been sort of hiding it . . . Obliged again to you for lending me a hand. When I see the rest of the boys tomorrow I'll tell them, too."

"Reckon we was all glad to help. Bert was a friend of us all."

Shawn, having put the dipper back on the bucket and tucked the hideaway gun once again under his belt inside his shirt, folded his arms across his chest and nodded to the two men.

"Then I think you ought to know right now who it was that killed him," he said coolly.

Tip shrugged. "We already know—was you or one of that bunch that kidnapped the Floods."

"You're wrong. It was the deputy here—or one of the outlaw gang. He's part of it."

Rufus and Tip exchanged glances and laughed. Carr joined in. "That's a good one," he said. "Man'll say about anything when he knows he's headed for a hanging."

"For sure," Tip agreed, and pushing Rufus before him, stepped through the doorway into the night.

Carr, face stolid, moved back to the door, glanced out, and then closing the panel, dropped the bar into place. Returning to the desk, he took up the bundle he had been carrying when he entered and placed it in the bottom of the gun rack.

"That the money?" Shawn asked quietly.

The deputy turned to him. "What money?"

"Don't give me that," Starbuck said scornfully. "I know it was you that bushwacked me. I followed the pinto's tracks right into town. You should've done a better job of killing me."

Carr settled on the corner of the desk. A dry smile pulled at his lips. "Reckon I should've at that, but it ain't over yet."

"Is for you. Little thing you overlooked—Lester had Mendoza and Frick riding herd on me. No doubt in my mind they saw you shoot me down, take the money . . . Little surprised they haven't moved in on you yet."

It was no more than a shot in the dark but it brought a frown to the lawman's features. After a moment he shrugged.

"That's a crock of bull—"

"You're wrong there. Nobody double-crosses Lester and gets away with it—Mendoza either. He's one I sure don't want dogging my trail."

"Can look after myself," Carr said with no great conviction in his voice. "Time they figure out what's happened, I'll be long gone."

"Fooling yourself. Like as not they're out there now watching that horse you got waiting. You try going to the saddle and you're a dead man."

"Oh, I reckon not—"

"One way to find out—try it!"

Jess Carr was silent for a long minute. He grinned. "Maybe that's a little job I'll let you do for me. If they gun you down I'll tell folks you got away from me, was trying to escape—and I shot you."

"Don't think that'll work. Lester and the others know us both—"

"Not if you're wearing my hat."

"Might work but you'll still have Lester and his bunch to deal with. Best thing you can do is turn the money over to me, let me carry it to them. That'll get you out of the hot grease and save the Floods, too."

Carr shook his head. "Nope, ain't nobody getting that money but me."

"You willing to risk your life for it?"

"You're goddamn right! Worth it for fifty thousand dollars . . . Stand up; I'm locking you in a cell while I do a little more thinking."

Shawn slowly got to his feet. The deputy's glance touched the empty holster on his hip, motioned toward the cells.

"Let's go—"

Starbuck wheeled indifferently, took a step toward the hallway, came back around fast. The hideaway pistol was leveled at Carr's middle.

"Now, we'll do it my way," Shawn said quietly. "Get your hands up."

The lawman raised his arms. Starbuck stepped in close, removed his weapon, glancing at it as he did. It was the same caliber as his own. He dropped it into his holster, replacing the pistol taken from him earlier by one of the posse members. Picking up the ring of keys, he pointed at the cells.

"Move—"

Muttering curses, Jess Carr started toward the hallway. Reaching the first cell, he halted, waited while Starbuck unlocked it, and then stepped inside. As the door clanged shut behind him, he turned.

"Was just thinking—you and me could make a deal. I'm willing to split that fifty thousand."

"Forget it," Starbuck replied, turning the key and dropping back to the office.

"Twenty-five thousand—that's a hell of a lot of money, cowboy—"

Shawn dropped the keys into the water bucket, bent hurriedly, and took the bundle from the gun rack's lower shelf. The covering was an old brush jacket, and through it he could feel the shape of the leather satchel. Ripping off the garment, he opened the bag, nodded in satisfaction. The money was there.

Tucking the satchel under an arm, he crossed to the window, glanced out, his ears closed to Carr's pleas to be reasonable, to not be a damned fool. The sorrel was standing at the hitchrack. Shawn turned at once, started for the door, halted as motion down the street caught his eye. He looked closer. It was Jimson and a half-a-dozen or more men. They were headed for the jail.

Taut, Starbuck pivoted, hurried toward the building's rear entrance. He would have to forget the sorrel for the moment. Reaching the back door, he slid the crossbar out of its brackets, allowed it to fall to the floor, and yanked open the thick panel. As he plunged out into the darkness behind the structure he heard Jess Carr's yell.

"Help! Jailbreak—help!"

18

Starbuck cut right as he bolted into the night, entered an alley. Racing along it he was aware of more shouting, this time from the street. Jimson and the men with him had heard the deputy, were now probably crowding through the doorway into the jail.

It was a bad break and he cursed himself for delaying too long. He could not reach the sorrel without being seen—and he could go nowhere without a horse. He recalled abruptly that Carr had left his mount somewhere behind the jail, slowed, looked over his shoulder. He saw the animal. It had been picketed to the left of the building—and he had turned away from it, to the right. He rushed on. It was too late now to double back. Jimson and the others would be hot on his trail in only moments. He'd get a horse at the livery barn—the one where Carr had stabled his pinto. It should be close by.

Keeping near the line of buildings, he rushed on. The yelling near the jail had increased as more men were summoned to the scene to aid in the pursuit. Likely they were having problems finding the keys to Carr's cell; the bucket of water was no ordinary place to hide them. Such would buy a little time for him. The fact, too, that the stable and the jail were at opposite ends of the town was also in his favor.

"There he goes!" a voice cried, and immediately the narrow alley rocked with the echoes of pistol shots.

It hadn't taken them long, Shawn thought grimly as bullets thudded into a board fence to his left and kicked up dirt around his feet. He broke stride, dodged to one side. More guns began to blast. A slug plucked at his sleeve, another clipped the brim of his hat—and he realized he'd never make it to the end of the alley alive.

He glanced about, desperately searching for cover. A narrow passageway separating two of the buildings was only steps away. It would lead him back to the street, somewhere near the town's center, but that was a worry he'd face when he got there. He was a dead man if he stayed where he was.

Bent low, he ducked into the dark weed- and trash-littered corridor, legged it for its opposite end. The men behind him were not yet aware that he had turned off, thanks to the shadows that filled the alley.

He came to the end of the passage, slowed. It would be a mistake to burst suddenly into view; best to enter the street casually, attempt to pass himself off as just another of the milling bystanders wondering what all the excitement was about.

Bracing himself, with the sound of the men in the alley pounding by only a few yards away, Starbuck eased onto the sidewalk. He sighed quietly. The street was deserted at this end, everyone abroad being congregated in front of the jail. Halting, he stepped into a darkened doorway. He needed a few moments to catch his breath and decide his next move.

The search party was now between him and the stable, thus he could forget about getting himself a horse from that source. But he could not remain where he was for long. Already the men in the alley would know they had overrun him somehow, would be hurrying back, making a thorough search along the buildings, front and rear.

Brushing at the sweat clothing his face, he glanced toward the jail. He could see the sorrel still at the rack. The crowd was thinning, apparently shifting to the alley for a better view of the activities. Two men were standing on the porch of a nearby building, their backs to him. Hope lifted within him. With a bit of luck he might be able to work his way along the street and get to the gelding.

He moved off at once, conscious of the long chance he was taking, aware also that the shooting in the alley had stopped. Jimson and the others had discovered he was not in front of them and were now backtracking. He hurried on, avoiding the lighted store windows as best he could, striving to not make himself obvious by too much haste. There were only three men in front of the jail now, all that remained of the crowd. The pair on the porch of the building opposite were still in evidence.

Starbuck drew to a halt at the corner of the structure adjacent to the lawman's quarters. In the flare of lamplight issuing from the window he studied the men leaning against the hitchrack. None were familiar, but he hadn't had a close look at all of the posse members.

"That's what the deputy's claiming." The voice of one reached Starbuck.

"Well, it sure don't say much for him—letting himself get locked up in his own jail," another commented.

"Got to remember this ain't a man like Bert Wilger we're talking about. This here's the deputy."

Shawn stirred impatiently. The sorrel was so near, yet with the three men standing at the rack no more than a stride from him, he might as well be at the far end of town.

Two men entered the street farther down, crossed over, and stepped up onto the porch fronting a saloon. Others appeared, joined them, some going on inside the building, a few pausing to converse. The search party was beginning to forsake the alley and reassemble. Odds were good all would report at the jail.

He had no choice but to take a chance. Waiting further could only end in disaster. Reaching down he made certain of the gun in his holster, moved out of the shadows into the open. Two of the men near the sorrel touched him with their glances, continued to talk. Walking slowly, indifferently, Shawn strolled across the front of the jail, paused to look inside as any curious bystander could be expected to do. There was no one inside the building, and he continued, angling toward the hitchrack and the sorrel.

Halting at the side of the gelding, nerves taut, grimly silent, Starbuck tugged at the reins slip-knotted around the crossbeam, freed them. Fighting the urge to vault onto the saddle and race away, he slipped a foot into the stirrup and swung onto the horse. At once the three men turned to him.

Hooking the handle of the satchel over the horn, he let his hand drop to his pistol. The movement, on Shawn's far side, went unnoticed by the men who continued to stare at him.

"That your animal?" one asked.

"You think I'd be climbing on him if he wasn't?" Starbuck snapped.

The man shrugged, glanced at his companions. "No, reckon maybe you wouldn't. Just wanted to say he's a mighty fine looking—"

The relief flowing through Starbuck was checked abruptly as a yell lifted from the porch of the saloon. A gunshot flatted through the night, and as Shawn wheeled the gelding and spurred for the darkness beyond the jail, more shouts went up.

"Hell—that was him!" one of the men now crouched low by the hitchrack said in a wild voice. "The killer!"

Shawn barely heard as he swept around the corner of the building and raced for a cluster of trees some distance ahead. There were no more shots but the yelling was coming closer. Likely the entire search party, with a few additions, was again on his trail.

But it would be a different story this time, he thought as the sorrel rushed on toward the trees. He would be out of sight before they even reached the alley. His problems with Bonnerville were over—at least for a while.

19

It was late—near midnight, Starbuck guessed—but he was getting off in good time. Barring any delays, he should be able to meet Cole Lester's deadline without difficulty. He would have a greater distance to travel, however, than when he had followed the Blackman Trail.

The outlaws would be looking for him on the road that led south out of Sante Fe since it was unlikely that they knew he had been forced to swing wide and go to Bonnerville. Thus he could figure on two, perhaps three hours of additional riding before he was in the area where he could expect to encounter Cruz Mendoza or Lonnie Frick.

He pushed on steadily, with the gelding showing signs of tiring as the miles dragged slowly by. He was in little better condition than the horse. Worn, hungry, and now that the tense minutes of excitement in the streets of the settlement were behind him, the pain in his head once more made itself known. But he gave it no consideration, pressed on doggedly.

The sun broke over the eastern horizon in a broad flare of color. It was quickly hot, it seemed to him, and the sorrel lagged even more. He began to worry about the big horse and halted frequently for short periods to rest him. If the gelding failed and he was set afoot, all would then be lost. He could not possibly walk the remaining distance in time—and the outlaws, despite Lester's promise, would not be looking for him that far south.

Late in the morning he reached a small, thin stream cutting a narrow path through a grove of trees. Halting, he dammed its course to form a pool the size of his hat and allowed the sorrel to satisfy his thirst. There was a sparse stand of grass nearby, and loosening the saddle cinch and slipping the bridle, he put the horse to grazing while he saw to his own needs.

When he was again on the move the gelding was considerably improved but what he really needed was a full night's rest, Shawn knew; it was something he could also use, along with a decent meal.

Noon found him crossing a broad flat that lay in the center of a circle of rocky hills. The sun was intense and the glare from the sand and shale caused him to pull his hat low over his eyes to minimize the discomfort, but he gave it little thought; he was on familiar ground now. He recalled that particular stretch of country and certain land formations. He had passed that way when he trailed Jess Carr to the settlement. The clearing where the holdup occurred was not too far ahead.

He reached that point around the middle of the afternoon, then began to veer west. Mendoza and Frick would be nearby now, he guessed, since he was moving into the area in which they were to await him—earlier bypassed when he was compelled to ride due south after the deputy. It was a full hour later, however, when motion in the brush along the trail caught his attention and shortly afterward the two outlaws put in their appearance.

The vaquero, a cold smile on his lips, watched Shawn draw to a halt. "You cut things close, senor."

"Got held up," Starbuck replied.

Frick eyed him suspiciously. "Where'd you come from? I didn't spot you topping out the rise."

Mentioning that he had been in Bonnerville wouldn't be wise, Starbuck decided; it could lead them to think he had gone there to enlist aid and was planning some sort of double-cross. And as for Jess Carr, he'd let that ride and see what developed.

"Took the wrong trail back up a ways," he said, and let it drop there.

Mendoza eased up beside him, lifted his pistol from its holster. Shawn merely nodded but his muscles had tightened quickly; if the vaquero searched him he would find the hideaway gun and the slight edge the weapon could give him would be gone. But Mendoza seemed satisfied, and shoving Starbuck's weapon under his belt, backed away.

"That the money?" Frick asked, pointing at the satchel. The scar on the outlaw's face showed white and there was a wildness in his eyes.

"That's it."

"I'll take it," Lonnie said, extending his hand.

Starbuck made no move to hand over the bag. Anger flushed the man's features.

"You hear? Give it to me!"

"I'm dealing with Lester," Shawn said. "Aim to turn it over to him—nobody else."

Mendoza shrugged, glanced at his partner. "It is better," he said quietly. "Do not worry, you will get your share. . . . We go."

There was a change in the Mexican. Shawn had become aware of it the moment the two outlaws had stopped him. The easy politeness he had earlier displayed was now icy, almost a sullenness.

He swung about, followed the vaquero into the brush, with Lonnie Frick pulling in behind him. They rode due west, pointing directly into the lowering sun. A while later the towering peaks and ridges of Blackman Mountain began to grow more definite, and Starbuck wondered if they were returning to the same location where he had been taken to meet the Floods. If so, the outlaws had not changed campsites.

Somewhere far to the south a gunshot sounded, the report hollow and faint. Mendoza paused to turn his eyes in the direction but he did not halt, judging the shot to be of no threat. It would be a posse from Bonnerville, Shawn reckoned, again searching for him. He wondered if Jess Carr would be heading up the party; if true, the riders would undoubtedly be steered well clear of the country into which Mendoza was leading him.

They broke out of the low brush country, entered an area of rolling foothills. The vaquero cut north, came shortly to a large arroyo that curved toward the nearby mountain. As they pursued it, it became steeper and narrower until it converted finally into a rugged canyon up which a trail wound its way. It would have been impossible to bring the wagon by that route and it was only logical to assume it was taken in from some different approach.

They climbed steadily for a half mile and then leveled off on a fairly large plateau. Mendoza took them across the flat toward a bank of red-faced buttes, and reaching there, he swung wide and doubled back up another path that led to the top of the formations. There Shawn saw a wide meadow, green with grass and dotted with trees. A narrow stream wound its way across the near side, disappeared in the distance.

Mendoza did not have to tell him they had

reached the camp. He spotted the wagon a few moments later in a grove.

"We have a *compadre* of yours," the vaquero said as they loped across the field toward the camp.

Starbuck frowned. "Who?"

"The old one who drives."

Frank Ogden! He understood now why he had seen nothing of the old man while he was in the settlement, but what was he doing—

Mendoza seemed to read his mind. "He come to find you, we find him."

"Was going to ride on but I sort've talked him out of it," Frick said with a laugh.

Ogden evidently had made inquiries at the livery stable that first day. On being told by the hostler that he had asked how to find the Blackman Trail, Frank had set out at once in the hope that he could be of help.

The meaning of Lonnie Frick's words suddenly registered. "He bad hurt?"

The outlaw grinned. "Oh, I reckon he'll live, leastwise for a spell."

Anger stirred through Starbuck. "He's an old man. Don't expect you found it much trouble to work him over."

"Not much," Frick replied. "Maybe you'd like to try your hand with me?"

"Going to look forward to it," Shawn said, and put his attention back to the camp.

Lester and Ed Jacks were standing near the dead coals of the fire. Orville Flood was moving toward them from the wagon. As he was looking, Carla climbed down from the vehicle, leaned against a rear wheel. There was no sign of Ogden; likely he was inside, out of the sun.

Tension gripped him as he pulled the sorrel to a halt before Lester. He was unsure of what to expect in those next few minutes—and he had no faith in the outlaw's promise to release them all when the ransom was in his hands.

"You get it?"

Shawn nodded, lifting the satchel by its handle for him to see.

Cole Lester reached out for it, frowned as Starbuck ignored the motion. He took a step nearer. "What's this all about?"

"Want to know where we—the Floods, Ogden, and myself—stand. We free to go when you get the money?"

Lester's face was a hard-cornered mask. "We'll talk about that later," he snapped. "Now, hand it over!"

20

Shawn heard the creak of leather, the thud of boot heels as Frick and Mendoza came off their horses, moved toward him. Orville Flood, his features strained, quickened his approach.

"Give it to him—give it to him!" he shouted.

Starbuck shrugged, tossed the satchel to the outlaw chief, and swung from his saddle. It was to be just as he had feared—Lester had no intentions of letting the Floods and him and Frank Ogden go free. Arms folded across his chest, he watched Lester open the bag, finger through the packs of currency and loose gold coins.

"Knew they'd pay," Flood said in a satisfied voice. "Told you they would."

Cole Lester nodded slowly. "Wish now I'd made it a hundred thousand."

Fear stirred through Shawn. It was an idea that had to be scotched quickly else the whole thing would start all over again.

"Doubt if you would have got it," he said. "Flood's brother wasn't too happy about forking over fifty thousand."

Lester raised his lifeless eyes to Orville, smiled thinly. "Guess we know better, don't we. You're worth plenty to him and his crowd."

"I'm his brother—"

The outlaw laughed. "Don't ask me to believe that means anything! Maybe you're forgetting I was working for Carl when this deal started hatching. I know the whole damned works—inside and out."

Starbuck glanced from the smirking face of Cole Lester to that of Flood, uneasy and twitching nervously. The other outlaws were listening indifferently but Carla had moved up to be within earshot.

"What deal?" Starbuck asked quietly.

"The one they've got going—one that depends on their getting Orville elected so's they can push through their plans for the *Pastizal*—"

Flood brushed eyes with Lester agitatedly. "Now—wait—"

"He's trotting around the country telling the suckers that turning over the *Pastizal* to that company of English lords and getting two hundred and fifty thousand dollars for it is a fine thing, that it'll be a big help to the Territory. You want to know how much they'll really get if they put it over?

"One million dollars, that's what! One million, and who pockets the difference? Why, Orville and big brother Carl and the rest of their crowd."

A gasp escaped Carla's lips. Flood glanced worriedly over his shoulder at her, and then shrugging, looked down.

"This true?" Starbuck asked.

Orville Flood made no reply. Lester closed the satchel with a snap, nodded. "You're goddamn right it's true, and he can't say it ain't!"

Anger whipped through Starbuck—anger at Flood, at the U.S. marshal who had brought him into contact with the man, at those who were behind him, and at himself for not being more careful and permitting himself to become a part of the fraud. He was stepping out of it right there and then; he'd look out for himself and Frank Ogden, somehow manage an escape from the outlaws—and let Orville Flood fend for himself and Carla.

Reason took over at the thought of the girl. He would quit but he couldn't leave Carla—or her father—at the mercy of Lester and the others. And he reckoned he couldn't blame the lawman who had gotten the job for him. Likely he was as unaware of what was going on as he had been. . . . But he'd have no more to do with it. He'd get the Floods safely to Bonnerville, the nearest town, if he could, and then ride on. Pulling off an escape, however, was not going to be any easy chore.

He turned to Lester. A beginning had to be made somewhere. "You've got your ransom. I've lived up to my end of the bargain—expect you to live up to yours."

"My end?" the outlaw said mildly. He shifted his attention to his partners, standing apart and passing a bottle of whiskey between them.

"What I mentioned before—turning us loose. I'd like to head out before dark."

Mendoza laughed. "You are in a hurry, senor?"

Shawn ignored the vaquero, waited for Lester's expected reply. He could feel the comforting pressure of the short barreled forty-one against his belly, but it would be a mistake to go for it now; he might bring down one or possibly two of the outlaws, but no more before the others got him.

"It's a little late to be pulling out," Lester said. "Wait till morning. Can talk about it then."

"What's the point?"

"Point is we ain't ready just yet to get moving. There's five of us in on this little shebang and the fifth won't be getting here until tonight. . . . Got to wait for him."

The fifth member—Jess Carr. Shawn gave that thought. There was small chance the deputy would show up to claim his share of the money, being certain that Lester and the other outlaws would be told of his attempt to take all of the ransom for himself. Starbuck considered the wisdom of now relating the incident, ruled against it. The longer the outlaws delayed their final departure, the more time he would have in which to come up with a plan for escape.

"Who—who?" He heard Orville Flood stammer.

"Just a good boy that helped us set this whole

thing up," Cole replied. "Done the inside work for us."

"Then—when he comes—are you letting us go?"

Lester smiled. "Like I told Starbuck there, we'll talk about it—in fact I'll be thinking it over all night."

Starbuck swore. "Why don't you just come out and tell him that you plan to kill us all?" he said in disgust. "You didn't back off murdering Bert Wilger. Adding four more to the list shouldn't be any sweat."

"Won't be," Lester replied evenly. "Just have to hold off until my friend Jess gets here. Got to know how things stand—where that posse'll be, things like that." He paused, looked closely at Shawn, nodded. "Yeah, Jess Carr. That don't seem to surprise you none."

"It doesn't," Starbuck said, and smiled grimly at the puzzled expression that filled the outlaw's eyes. But he let his answer go unexplained.

Cole glanced at the setting sun. "Getting dark. Might as well settle down for the night. Going to be the same as before—you'll all be tied to the wagon—"

"'Cepting the gal," Lonnie Frick broke in, eying Carla hungrily.

Lester paused, considered all three of his partners with faint disdain, and shrugged. "Like for you to save a bit of that whiskey," he said.

"Figured we might do a little celebrating tonight."

"Got another quart in my saddlebags," Ed Jacks assured him promptly.

"Good. . . . See that you hang onto it," Lester ordered, and switched back to Orville Flood, who was listening to all that was being said in stunned silence.

"No sense taking it so hard, Orvy! You went out on a limb and it broke off. Now, if things'd worked out you'd be a rich man. They didn't so you're a dead one. Was a gamble and you lost."

Flood found his voice. "Still—still no cause to murder us!"

Cole Lester smiled. "Plenty of cause—fifty thousand dollars worth," he corrected bluntly, and turned away.

21

Starbuck, brushing by Flood and Carla, crossed to the wagon. He heard Frick call to him, but paying no attention, he pulled himself up onto the tailgate of the vehicle and peered into its shadowy interior.

"Frank?"

The figure sprawled out on the wagon's bed stirred slightly. "Yeah?" The word was spoken low, sounded thick.

"It's me—Starbuck."

Ogden drew himself to a sitting position. Shawn recoiled in horror. The driver's face was a misshapen, purple mass. Both eyes were swollen shut, his lips were double their normal size, and the lobe of his left ear had been torn loose and now hung limply against his neck. His nose was broad, appeared twisted. In the failing light the man's face was a grotesque mask.

"My God!" Starbuck muttered. "Frick do all this to you?"

Ogden raised a shaky hand to his head, gingerly touched the bandaged area over his left temple. "Come looking for you, figuring I could maybe help. End up being a care," he said, speaking with difficulty. "Sure did give me a working over, didn't he?"

"Hardly the word for it. Why?"

"Can't rightly say, unless he was just wanting to show hisself off. Reckon he wanted to prove what a big man he was to the gal."

"Carla? What did she have to do with it?" Shawn asked, fighting to control the anger that gripped him.

"Nothing, far as she's concerned. But he's been sort of after her, trying to get cozy, make a hit with her and the like. You all right?"

"Got myself nicked, that's all."

"Shot? By who?"

"Jess Carr. He's part of the Lester outfit. . . . Tell you about it after we get out of here."

He hesitated. There was movement of some sort just outside the wagon.

"We leaving?" Ogden said, voice lifting a little.

"Hope so," Shawn replied, unwilling to say more. "You stretch out there and take it easy."

"Sure, sure—just ain't much else I can do, shape I'm in," Frank replied, sinking back onto his pallet. "That little gal, she's all right, Shawn. Was her that pulled Frick off me—scared as she is of him."

"I'll remember that—and Frick, too," Starbuck said, moving to back out of the wagon. He paused, feeling a hand grip him by the ankle.

"Come on, you!" It was Lonnie Frick's voice. "Get yourself all tied up nice to the wheel."

Shawn kicked himself loose of the man's

fingers, dropped to the ground. At once the outlaw shoved the barrel of a pistol into his spine, jabbed viciously.

"Go ahead!" he invited in a harsh whisper. "Just aching for you to start something. Cole don't want no shooting on account of that posse, but I reckon if I had to do it he wouldn't mind."

Shawn curbed the fury surging through him. He'd like nothing better than to spin, knock away the weapon pressed against him with an elbow, and then beat the outlaw into a pulp. But to do so would be a mistake, would void the plan that was shaping up in his mind. Later he would have his time with Lonnie Frick—and Frick would pay for every blow he'd dealt Frank Ogden.

"Over there—" the outlaw directed, shoving with the gun's barrel.

Starbuck moved up to the rear wheel of the wagon. Orville Flood was being trussed to the one forward by Mendoza. Beyond them Carla watched, her features barely distinguishable in the rising darkness.

The vaquero completed his job on Flood, moved to where he faced Shawn. "You will spread the legs and the arms, senor," he said.

Shawn complied silently as Mendoza bound each of his ankles to a spoke, his hands to the rim of the wheel. When he was finished he looked up, smiled, and reaching inside Starbuck's shirt, drew out the pistol hidden there.

"You have secrets, eh, my friend?" he asked in a bantering voice as he held up the weapon for Frick to see.

Lonnie swore. "The damn tricker!" he shouted, and swung a knotted fist at Shawn's jaw.

Starbuck jerked away, took a glancing blow on the neck. Disappointment was heavy within him. As long as he had the forty-one their chances for completing an escape were good, but all was not hopeless yet—at least it wasn't if the outlaws didn't search him further.

Frick jerked the belly gun from the vaquero's fingers, thrust it under his own belt. "Always figured to get me one of these."

Mendoza studied the scar-faced man for a long moment, his mouth a tight, down-curving line, and then shrugging moved off toward the center of the camp where Cole Lester was building a fire. On beyond him Shawn could see Ed Jacks busy at tying the horses to a picket line stretched between two trees.

Lonnie scrubbed at his mouth, flung a glance at Carla, and said, "I'll be coming back for you later, honey," then swaggered off to join Lester and the vaquero, now digging into a box for the food they would use for the evening meal.

Carla waited until the outlaw had squatted beside the others, then stepped hurriedly to her father's side.

"Papa—are you all right? I saw him hit—"

"I'm not hurt," Flood answered in a windy voice. He looked closely at the girl. "Carla, I'm sorry—sorry you had to find out, sorry that I've gotten you into this mess—"

"Never mind," she said. "What's done is done," and she looked imploringly at Starbuck. "Is there any hope? With them finding that pistol on you—"

"Was a bad break of luck but I figure I can still manage," Shawn said. "Going to take a little help from you."

She threw a glance at the outlaws. All four were now gathered around the fire. Two spiders and a large coffee pot were now propped over the flames, and Mendoza was slicing potatoes into one of the pans. The sound of meat beginning to fry was coming from the other. Nearby Ed Jacks was taking another swig at his bottle, almost empty.

"I'll do what I can," she said, "but I don't see—"

"Want you to go with Frick when he comes to get you."

Carla drew back, her face barely visible in the darkness. "No!"

Orville Flood drew himself up stiffly. "I'll not permit that! I'll not let you sacrifice my daughter for the sake of the rest of us!"

Starbuck shifted his position, striving to ease the strain on his legs and shoulders. "Don't intend to let her get hurt," he said stiffly.

"Then how—"

Shawn ignored the man, fixed his attention on the girl. "I carry a knife inside my boot—the left one. Soon as it's darker I want you to get it. You can make out like you're adjusting the rope around my ankle like maybe it's hurting me some."

Carla nodded.

"When you get it, cut the ropes that are around my wrists, then put the knife in my hand. I'll hang onto the wheel so's they won't notice I'm loose—"

"What about your ankles? Hadn't I better cut those ropes, too?"

"No, I'll do it later. Be hard to keep my legs up against the wheels without them being tied to it."

"I see. Then what?"

"When Frick comes after you, go with him. Put up a little fight. He's expecting it, but give in. Think you can handle it?"

The girl trembled visibly. "I—I guess so. Where'll you be?"

"Only a few steps behind you. Soon as he goes off with you, I'll follow. Should be right away unless one of the others happens to be watching. Anyway, I'll get to you fast as I can. Be up to you to do a little fighting with him, keep him busy until I'm there."

"But what if you can't follow?"

"No reason why I won't be able to. Might be right away, or it could be a couple of minutes, but I'll be there—not only for your sake but on account of Frank Ogden. Little score to settle for him . . . Got it all straight?"

Carla appeared to have regained control of herself. She gave him a small, tight smile. "I'm frightened—but I'll do my part."

He nodded to her. She was a changed woman, far different from the one he had met only a short time ago.

"Expect you will. Once we've taken care of Frick we'll be that much closer to getting out of here."

"I know, but he'll only be the start. There's three others, Shawn, how can you handle them?"

It was the first time she had ever called him by his given name. "Not sure. I've got no plan for that. All I can do is let things happen and try to turn them our way. Lot depends on getting Frick out of the picture without stirring up the others."

"I understand—"

"Big thing for you is to not worry about it. Just do what I tell you and leave the rest to me."

"Starbuck—"

Shawn's jaw hardened as he turned his eyes to Flood. "Yeah?"

"Want you to know I'm grateful," the man said, struggling briefly against the ties that pinned him to the wagon wheel as he sought to lessen the discomfort. "All this you're doing for us is—"

"My job," Starbuck cut in coldly. "Once I get you back to Bonnerville, I'm through. You're on your own from there."

22

The fire had dwindled to a few small, flickering flames. Ed Jacks had been the first to give way to sleep, and he now lay sprawled in the shadows just beyond the shrinking flare of light. Mendoza was next, and now Cole Lester was showing signs of calling it a day. Only Lonnie Frick, hunched nearby, nursing the last of the liquor in the bottle that had passed freely between the outlaws, appeared to be fully awake.

Muscles aching from the spread-eagle position into which he had been forced, Starbuck watched the two men narrowly. If he had Lester figured correctly, the outlaw chief would cross to the wagon, make an inspection to assure himself that all was secure with his prisoners before allowing himself to sleep. After that Frick could be expected to make his move.

"About time," he said in a low voice. "You awake?"

Carla, in her blanket placed under the wagon, reached through the spokes of the wheel and touched the back of his leg. "I am."

"Like as not Lester will pay us a call to be sure your pa and I are still tied. Once he's done that and is back over there, then I want you to get my knife and cut my hands loose."

"I'll be ready."

Shawn shifted again, swore quietly. His shoulders throbbed and he felt numb from the waist down. "They been tying your pa up this way every night?" he asked, glancing at Flood.

"No. Before they just took rope and bound his hands to the wagon tongue. . . . Is he all right?"

Starbuck looked again at Orville Flood. His head hung forward and his body hung limply against the bonds that linked him to the wheel.

"Asleep, I think," he replied.

She was silent for a time. Then, "Shall I cut him free, too?"

"Best you don't," he said quickly. "Could make a wrong move, give us away."

"He's suffering so. I'll warn him to be careful."

Starbuck gave it thought. There was no doubt Flood was in pain, but he had little faith in the man's judgment and preferred that he be where he could do no harm or get in the way.

"Won't be for much longer, if things work out. If they don't, it won't make any difference. . . . Careful."

Lester had risen to his feet. He had not parted with the satchel of money since the moment it was delivered to him, now had it tucked under an arm. Glancing at Frick he said something, then turned and started leisurely across the strip of open ground that separated the camp from the wagon.

Shawn allowed his head to drop, and feigning sleep, waited. He heard Lester move in close, felt his fingers as they checked the ropes binding his arms to the wheel. Satisfied, he moved on to Flood, went through the same procedure. Eyes barely open, Starbuck watched him look into the wagon, pivot, peer under the vehicle at Carla, and then head back toward the fire.

"Get the knife," Shawn murmured.

At once Carla's hand was inside his boot, probing for the blade carried there. She drew back. Her low whisper came to him.

"I have it."

Starbuck, his attention on Lester, waited until the outlaw had reached the camp. The fire was little more than ashes, and in the near darkness both men were only shadows. Lester bent over, began to shake out his blanket.

"Now—"

At the word the girl slipped silently from beneath the wagon, and moving swiftly, sliced through the rope that bound his left arm to the wheel, and then the one pinning the right. Shawn felt the hilt of the knife press into his open palm, the light touch of her hair against his face as she passed by him, and then she was once again under the vehicle.

"Good, good," he whispered, gripping the wheelrim tight to maintain his position.

Lester had laid out his blanket, was dropping

onto it. He had chosen a spot well back from the others and now was scarcely visible in the darkness. Frick had not stirred, was yet hunched by the dead fire. Mendoza and Ed Jacks slept soundly. If there had been any wondering as to why Jess Carr had not put in an appearance, there had been no evidence of it. Likely they had given him up for the night and assumed he would arrive in the morning.

Orville Flood groaned, swayed against his bonds, fell quiet. A small sound came from Carla's throat.

"I'll cut him loose as soon as I can," Shawn reassured the girl. "Be safer where he is for a while. When you fed Frank was he any better?"

"Some," she said in a low voice. "Eyes are still swollen shut but he doesn't seem to hurt so . . . That was a terrible thing—the way Frick kept hitting him, even when he was unconscious and on the ground."

Her voice broke as her own fears overcame her. Starbuck, not taking his eyes off the outlaw, said, "You'll be fine—I'll see to that. Don't worry about him."

"I—I guess I can't help it. He's such a horrible man—an animal—"

"That's a bad thing to say about the animals," Shawn said. "An insult to them, I figure. If you—"

His words broke off. Lonnie Frick had abruptly gotten to his feet. Standing there, he tipped the bottle to his lips, drained it, and then hurled the empty container off into the night. Wheeling, he started across the open ground.

"He's coming," Starbuck warned softly.

Again he heard a faint, stifled moan come from the girl. She was going through hell, he knew, and if there had been any other means for gaining escape available, he would not have subjected her to such terror. But Lonnie Frick's lust was their only chance; he hoped she would understand that and not feel too bitter toward him.

"When he takes you, fight him like I said, but try to work him around to where the wagon will be between you and the others. That'll keep them from seeing anything if somebody wakes up."

"I'll try—"

"You'll do fine—don't worry," Starbuck said once more, and allowed his head to again slump, his eyes to close as he pretended sleep.

Everything could go wrong in those next few moments. If Frick decided to examine the ropes about his wrists, too, he'd have no course left open but to strike with his knife and face the remaining outlaws, certain to be awakened by the commotion. Lonnie, he was sure, however, would waste no time on such unimportant items. His mind would be filled solely with thoughts of Carla and what lay ahead for him; besides, Cole Lester had looked them all over, and had satisfied himself that all was well.

The thump of the outlaw's boot heels ceased. Through slitted eyes Shawn saw Frick's dark shape loom close, bend down as he reached for the girl.

"No—" he heard her cry softly.

"Come on now," Lonnie said in a rough voice. "You been waiting for me—own up to it."

Starbuck's jaw set as he heard the scuffling sound of Carla being dragged from beneath the wagon. The urge to strike out, to bury the knife that he clutched in Frick's body, was almost overwhelming, but he fought it off, waited. His moment would come.

23

Head down, Shawn hung motionless in the darkness. To his right, and from the corner of an eye, he could see the blurred shapes of Frick and the girl as they moved off, struggling, into the darkness. Carla was twisting and writhing, flailing at the outlaw's head with both her fists. Frick was laughing quietly.

But Starbuck's attention was focused more on the men scattered about near the lifeless fire. Neither Cruz Mendoza nor Ed Jacks had stirred. He could not be certain, however, of Lester. The area where he had laid his bed was in the deep shadows, and Shawn, straining to see while the scraping noise of Carla being half dragged, half carried off into the brush grated in his ears, could only guess as to whether or not the outlaw leader had been aroused by Frick's activities and was sitting up watching.

Anxiety clawed suddenly at his throat. There was only silence on the far side of the wagon. He could hold off no longer, would simply have to risk it. Shaking his arms, he threw off the severed ropes, and bending forward slashed those that bound his legs to the spokes of the wagon wheel. He went to his knees at the abrupt release, hung there tensely. There was no warning yell from Lester.

Immediately he pivoted, ducked under the wagon, and came out between the opposite wheels. Slipping the knife back into its boot sheath, he listened into the darkness. The rattle of displaced gravel on ahead reached him. At once he hunched low, ran toward the sound.

He was on a slope, he realized, one spotted with clumps of brush and that led down into an arroyo. Grim satisfaction rolled through him. Frick had chosen a place well hidden from the camp and at a distance that precluded any sound reaching it.

He reached the edge of the sandy wash, paused, again listened into the moonless night. A faint cry of desperation brought him about. Carla and Frick were to his left—and still on the slope. Shawn moved hurriedly out into the arroyo, veered sharply, and followed its bank a dozen yards. Swaying shapes appeared abruptly above him. Silent, he mounted the low wall of the arroyo, closed in on the pair.

"Frick!"

At the sound of his name being spoken, the outlaw released his grasp on the girl, whirled. Starbuck, savage as a hunting cat, sprang at the man, caught him by the arms, and spinning about, threw him bodily into the wash.

He had a quick glimpse of Carla, her face a pale oval in the darkness, her hands fumbling to gather up the shreds of her torn dress as he pivoted, launched himself after the outlaw.

Frick, struggling to rise, to draw the pistol he wore, went down as Starbuck crashed into him, drove him flat against the sand. Shawn, clawing for the man's weapon, jerked it from its holster and threw it back up the slope in the direction of the girl. His hands then went searching for the hideaway gun the outlaw had appropriated earlier. It was not under his belt, had fallen to the ground somewhere.

All thoughts of it fled Starbuck's mind as the outlaw, over his surprise and shock, lashed out with a booted foot, caught him in the groin. Gasping with pain, Shawn rocked back, and then as fury overcame all else, he lunged again at the man, pulling himself upright.

They went down together, locked tight. Starbuck jerked an arm loose, drove a smashing blow into Frick's head, tried to free his other hand for a follow-up to the belly. Frick twisted onto his side, scrambled clear, spun as Shawn crowded in after him. Striking out blindly, he caught Starbuck squarely on the jaw with a wild right, sent him staggering back.

Curses leaping from his lips, he rushed in, fists cocked. Starbuck, brain still cobwebby from the blow, continued to pull away, instinctively following the admonitions of his father, Hiram, an expert in the art of fisticuffs who had tutored both him and his brother to a point of near perfection.

You get hit square and don't know whether you're coming or going, pull off, get your senses back. Ain't no shame in that, only smartness!

It was advice he'd never forgotten, and more than once it had served him well. Now, head clearing as he continued his retreat, he began to make it work further for him. Lowering his arms, he staggered, seemed to trip, almost go down. Frick swore loudly, surged toward him. Shawn jerked aside, and as the outlaw rushed by, smashed a left into the man's unprotected jaw, sent him to his knees.

Frick was up instantly. He whirled, both fists fanning the air. The outlaw's lips were pulled back over his teeth, and his eyes were wild. There was a smear of blood under his nose, more on the hair-matted chest, exposed when the buttons of his shirt had been ripped off.

"Goddamn you!" he muttered in a strangled voice.

The remembrance of what Frick had done to Ogden, of the horror and fright he had put Carla through, of the pain and bullying he had inflicted upon all, came again to Shawn's mind. A blinding rage soared through him as he rushed to meet the man.

But once more old Hiram's teachings laid their caution upon him. *Don't let nothing rile you, boy, when you're fighting. You let yourself get mad— you're beat.*

Starbuck slowed, lowered his head. His left arm shot out. Frick recoiled, rocked off balance as Shawn's fist met his hunched shoulder. As he half spun, Starbuck's right crossed, nailed him solidly on the jaw. The outlaw wilted, recovered slightly. Shawn smashed another left into his face, staggered him with a second right.

Methodically, mercilessly, Starbuck began to cut the outlaw to ribbons. Arms working like precisely guided pistons, he stabbed, jabbed and hammered Frick relentlessly about the head. The outlaw's hands dropped, hung limply at his sides. Legs spread, he swayed back and forth as Shawn, the memory of Frank Ogden's battered face before him, continued to exact his price.

Frick began to sink, going back on his haunches, then buckling forward. Starbuck caught him with his left hand, lifted him partly, knocked him sprawling with a hard right. Silent, breathing hard, he stepped up to the man, caught him by the shirt front, and dragged him upright. Again he drove the man to the floor of the arroyo.

"Oh—dear God—no!"

At the sound of Carla Flood's voice, he paused. The brittle calmness began to flow from him and he turned to her. She was looking down at the battered, bloody pulp of Lonnie Frick's features, both hands spread over her eyes as if she wished to shut out the sight.

"Not that—again," she cried softly, reliving

once more the frightful scene when the outlaw had set upon Frank Ogden.

"It's done," Starbuck said, putting his arm about her and turning her away. There was no apology in him for the punishment he had visited upon the man, only a grim sort of satisfaction.

Chafing his skinned and bruised knuckles, he moved hurriedly with the girl up the slope of the arroyo. In the heat of the moment he had all but forgotten Cole Lester and the others; now the urgency to face them and get finished—win or lose—pressed him.

A faint glint of metal on the ground caught his attention. Reaching down, he recovered the pistol he'd taken from Frick and tossed onto the slope. A step farther on he found the hideaway gun, half buried after it had fallen from the outlaw's belt and been stepped on.

Carla, too, had put the previous minutes behind her and was now thinking of what lay ahead. She caught at his arm.

"Had I better get those ropes, tie him?" she asked, pointing toward the arroyo.

"Later," Shawn replied, knocking the loose dirt from the forty-one and thrusting it inside his shirt. "He'll be right there for a spell." He raised his glance toward the camp. "You hear anything up there while I was . . . busy?"

She shook her head. "Nothing. I was afraid they might hear you and Frick, though."

"Sand sort of kept things quiet," he said. "Not much afraid of Ed Jacks or Mendoza hearing anything. Both pretty drunk. Was Lester I worried about, but since he didn't show up I guess we didn't rouse him."

Reaching out he took her hand in his, began to climb the slope quietly. "We get to the wagon," he said, lowering his voice, "you're to climb inside, and stay. The rest's up to me."

"I can help—you can let me have one of those pistols—"

"Feel better if I know you're where you won't get hurt. Job you did of getting Frick away from camp so's I could get to him is all I'm asking of you. You did fine."

They had reached the top of the slope. The wagon was just ahead, and beyond it the small clearing in which the outlaws slept. Starbuck pressed the girl's hand, pointed at the canvas-topped vehicle.

"Remember—stay inside," he whispered, and moving away from her, began to circle toward the sleeping men.

24

On hands and knees, taking advantage of every clump of brush, Starbuck made his way along the fringe of the clearing. He could barely make out the figure of Ed Jacks in the darkness. It was no more than a lumpy blur a short distance below the dead fire, and would be the first he would come to as he drew in close.

He was still unsure of Cole Lester, and not knowing whether or not the outlaw chief was awake troubled him. It would be like the man to sit back there in the night, watching and waiting for the proper moment to show himself and bring an end to the escape that was underway. But delaying the attempt because of uncertainty was out of the question; Starbuck knew he must gamble, push the small advantage that he had gained.

Halting behind a clump of mahogany, Shawn peered ahead. Jacks, snoring evenly, was little more than an arm's length away. A dozen paces farther on he could see Cruz Mendoza. The vaquero also appeared to be sleeping soundly but with much less gusto than his outlaw partner.

He tried again to locate Lester, drawing on his recollection of an hour or so earlier when he had watched the man lay out his blankets. Cole had chosen a place well beyond the fire—and somewhat to the north of the other men.

Satisfaction stirred Starbuck as his probing gaze settled finally on the outlaw's shape. Near a hedgelike stand of bushes, he was farther to the left than Shawn had thought, almost on a line with the picketed horses vaguely outlined nearby.

Starbuck lay back, considered the feasibility of simply rising, walking into the open, and challenging the three outlaws. He had two guns with which to do it—and in daylight it probably would work. But at night, with the outlaws widely separated, it would be risky, particularly where Lester was concerned. The man could duck quickly into the brush, and thus concealed by darkness, gain the upper hand. . . . It would be better to follow the course open to him, that of overcoming the outlaws one by one.

Carefully, quietly, Shawn moved to Ed Jacks' side. The outlaw lay on his back, mouth open, arms flung wide. Pulling Jacks' pistol from the holster still thonged to the man's leg, Shawn thrust it under his own belt. Drawing his knife, he cut the rawhide strip from the oiled leather pocket that had held the weapon, and turning to Jacks, rolled him slowly onto his side, then to his belly.

Half aroused, the outlaw snorted, gagged, started to raise his head. Starbuck had hoped to bind his wrists without disturbing him. Reaching for his pistol he took it by the barrel, waited. Jacks continued to stir, wheezing and coughing. Farther over Cruz Mendoza showed signs of awakening.

Shawn delayed no longer. Swinging the pistol swiftly, he struck the outlaw a sharp blow on the head. Ed Jacks went limp, face buried in the loose dirt. Taking the length of rawhide, Starbuck bound the man's wrists together, finishing off the chore by tying a bandana over his mouth and effectively silencing him.

Crouched low, he put his attention on the vaquero. Once Mendoza was taken care of, he would be faced with the fairly long distance that separated him from Lester. It would be best to play it safe, approach the outlaw leader carefully, as he had Jacks and Mendoza. He couldn't account for the feeling, but he was still not fully convinced that Cole Lester was asleep. But that was something he would face once the vaquero was out of it; going up against Lester alone, and certain there was no one left to move in on him from behind, would pose no—

Starbuck hunched lower beside Ed Jacks. There was movement near the hedge of bushes. Lester was stirring, sitting up. Either he had not been asleep, or for some reason had just awakened. Shawn frowned. He would have to change his plans, figure another way. If he could have gotten to Mendoza, put him out of action, as he had Jacks and Lonnie Frick, before Cole Lester roused, it would have made no difference. Now. . . .

The outlaw chief got slowly to his feet, making no sound; he was only a dark shadow in the night. He began to move away, fade into the background. He was going to the horses, Shawn realized, either to see to their security, or to mount one and depart.

Starbuck drew his legs under him, prepared to rise. If Lester had it in mind to pull out, it was because he wanted all of the ransom money for himself, which in itself was of little interest to Shawn; what did matter was that Lester was not only part of an outlaw gang that had murdered, but its leader, and as such had to be brought to justice. Kidnapping, too, was a crime, and to those charges they all must be made to answer. He would have to stop Cole Lester, prevent his escaping.

Turning, he crawled, belly flat on the ground, toward a thicker stand of brush to his right. By gaining it, he should be able to cut through the trees, come in on the horses from the rear. Reaching the clumps of rabbit bush and oak, he paused, looked back—froze.

Cruz Mendoza was drawing himself upright, his eyes turned to Lester, now standing among the picketed mounts. The vaquero hung there in the gloom, a half-bent, threatening shape, and then slowly he began to move forward.

Starbuck at once continued on, keeping pace with the vaquero but well to the side and in the deep brush. It should work to his favor; he would have both outlaws together, and capturing them should be easy. He halted, glanced toward the Mexican. The outlaw was no longer in view, blocked from sight by a weed-covered mound of earth. Or could he have worked his way into the heavy growth immediately ahead? Shawn studied the dense underbrush. It was possible; Cruz could have circled the mound hurriedly, ducked into the cover of scrub oak and other shrubs. If so, he would put himself directly behind Cole Lester.

"You leave us, *amigo*?"

The vaquero's laconic question was like a gunshot breaking a deep silence.

Starbuck moved forward quickly, drew up behind the first of the trees, a large cottonwood. The horses were a dozen yards away, and as he looked he saw Lester turn easily, deliberately, to face Mendoza at the edge of the clearing.

"Just looking things over," Cole said lazily. "Don't want none of the animals getting loose."

"So . . . It is necessary that you saddle your horse for such? I think you lie, *amigo*."

"Could be," Lester replied, and dipping sideways, drew his pistol and fired.

The rap of Mendoza's gun was so close that the two shots were almost as one, and the short stabs of flame spurting from the muzzles of their weapons appeared to reach for each other.

Starbuck moved forward, saw Lester stagger away from the nervously shying horses, fall, the satchel of ransom money clutched in one hand, pistol in the other. Mendoza, on his knees, head slung forward on his bowed shoulders, faced him from the edge of the clearing.

"I never trust you, *gringo ca—*" he began and abruptly toppled.

Motionless, Shawn stood by the cottonwood, the acrid bite of gunsmoke in his nostrils, the dying echoes of the reports in his ears. After a brief time he stirred, shook off the restraint that death coming violently to any man always laid upon him, and moved out into the open. Carla and the others at the wagon would have heard the shots, would now be wondering about their meaning, perhaps fearing for him. He'd see first to Mendoza and Lester; they were dead, he was certain, but he had to know.

Stopping at the side of the vaquero, he knelt, rolled him to his back. Cole's bullet had smashed into his chest. At such close range it had done terrible damage to the man; it was a miracle he had survived those few moments during which he had expressed his feelings toward the outlaw leader.

Rising, Starbuck crossed to Lester. He had died instantly, the vaquero's bullet tearing into his heart, and as in the case of his own slug, creating awesome havoc. Prying the handle of the satchel free of the outlaw's stiffening fingers, he drew himself erect. The horses had quieted and the only reminders now of the shooting were the two bodies and the still-lingering smell of burnt powder. Far over on Blackman Mountain a coyote barked, and shortly an answer came from the flats below, the sound lonely and fitting to the moment.

Hooking the satchel under an arm, Starbuck wheeled, started to double back across the open ground for the wagon. He pulled up short, a gusty sigh breaking from his lips. Jess Carr, pistol leveled, was facing him. He swore silently; he'd forgotten about the deputy, had carelessly written him off as no longer a factor since it was not likely, after his attempted double-cross of his partners, that he would show up at the camp.

"Obliged to you for saving me the trouble," Carr said. "Hadn't figured out how I was going to get that bag away from Cole and the others. Seems you done it for me."

Starbuck shook his head. "I never gunned them."

"No? Was between them, then? Expect Cole was trying to run out . . . Well, don't mean nothing now . . . Want you to just drop that bag right there, then back away."

Shawn released his grip on the satchel, allowed

it to fall. The wagon lay on beyond the deputy, its round, canvas top barely visible in the dark, but there was small chance of help coming from that point; Frank Ogden was unable to see, possibly could not walk. Orville Flood was still bound to one of the wheels, and Carla, by his own strict orders, was confined to the vehicle.

"Now, come here. Slow and easy. Keep your hands up where I can see them."

Starbuck raised his arms to where they were well away from his body, moved forward in careful, unhurried steps, his mind functioning coolly. That Carr intended to kill him was apparent, evidently believing that since there was no sign of anyone else around, he was now the remaining member of the kidnapping party.

As he approached the deputy, he could see the man glance at the pistol in its holster and then to the one taken from Ed Jacks and thrust under his belt. A faint smile pulled at his lips as if he were remembering something that would not be overlooked a second time.

"Far enough," he said.

Shawn halted. Jess Carr closed in cautiously, plucked the pistol from under his belt and threw it off into the brush. Reaching out again, he lifted the other from its holster, flung it aside also.

"Start walking—"

Starbuck nodded tightly. "In the back, that the way it's to be?"

"It makes a difference?" Carr asked, his smirk broadening.

"No, reckon not. Was how you got Bert Wilger, I expect."

"Wasn't me, was the vaquero done it . . . Walk . . ."

Shawn lowered his arms, began to move away from the man. On his third step he slipped his hand unnoticed inside his shirt for the forty-one. On the fourth he spun, triggered the short-barreled weapon.

Surprise and shock distorted Carr's face, impact drove him to the ground. He tried to rise as Starbuck returned to him, struggling briefly before he gave it up and lay quiet. Bending over, Shawn brushed the man's pistol out of reach, looked down at him. There was a puzzled, almost hurt expression in the deputy's eyes.

"Was—was it that damned belly gun—again?"

Starbuck nodded.

Jess Carr sighed heavily. "Figured I was pulling it when—" he began, and suddenly went limp.

For a long minute Shawn did not move, his eyes on the dead outlaw, and then reaching down he recovered the satchel of ransom money and started for the wagon. He'd turn it over to Orville Flood, and when morning came, they would all head back for the settlement.

25

It was late the afternoon of the following day when they reached Bonnerville. A crowd began to collect at once as the grim cavalcade pulled to a halt in front of the jail. Shawn and Carla Flood, along with the two outlaws Frick and Ed Jacks, were astride horses. The bodies of Lester, Cruz Mendoza, and Jess Carr were inside the wagon being driven by Frank Ogden. Flood was on the seat beside him, and the extra mounts were tied to the rear of the vehicle.

A new lawman, evidently appointed by the town council to fill the vacancy caused by Wilger's death, bustled out to meet them. He pulled up short, eyes on Starbuck.

"Say—ain't you—"

Shawn, hands resting on the horn of his saddle, only shrugged. The steadily enlarging crowd was swarming closer, shouting questions at Flood and Ogden, staring at the battered features of the driver and Lonnie Frick.

"Hey, Tom—you better have a look-see in the back of this here wagon!"

At the summons the deputy hurried to the rear of the vehicle. He returned shortly, and hand riding the butt of his pistol, again fixed his gaze on Starbuck.

"One of them bodies is Jess Carr," he said.

"They was going to 'point him sheriff here today. Want to know what—"

"Would've been a poor choice," Starbuck said dryly. "He was one of the kidnapping bunch."

A new rash of questions broke out. Orville Flood got to his feet, began to answer as best he could. Glancing about, Shawn began to recognize a few familiar faces in the assembly—Jimson, the man called Tip, Rufus, some that were familiar but that he had not heard called by name. The deputy said something and several men crowded up to Jacks and Lonnie Frick, dragged them off their horses, and hustled them into the jail. Flood was continuing his explanations, and Frank Ogden, having climbed down from the wagon seat, was surrounded by a group on the sidewalk.

Roweling the sorrel gently, Shawn pulled away from the rack and rode the short distance back up the street to the restaurant. He was bone-weary, hungry—and disgusted. The job that was to pay so well, providing him with enough cash to carry him for many months in the search for Ben, hadn't worked out at all. It had been no more than a waste of time.

Dismounting, he wrapped the sorrel's reins about the crossbeam of the rack, and entering the café, sat down at one of the tables. He'd have himself a meal, and then after collecting his gear at the hotel, ride on. There was no reason to stay in Bonnerville.

He gave his order to a tight-lipped waitress. It was filled and served promptly, he being the only patron, and within a few minutes he had finished it and was again on the street. Mounting the porch of the Western Star he paused to glance toward the jail. The crowd was still there but the wagon had been driven away, probably to the town's undertaker. There was no sign of Ogden or the Floods.

Entering the hotel's lobby, he moved toward the desk. Ernie Quinn, unaware apparently of what was taking place at the jail, was leafing through a catalog of some kind. He looked up. Startled, he sprang to his feet.

"Now, wait—"

"Came after my belongings," Starbuck said coldly, ignoring the man's fright.

Quinn bobbed, hurriedly passed the necessary key and stepped back. Mounting the stairs, Shawn went to the room he and Frank Ogden had shared, gathered together what was his, and returned to the lobby. Dropping the key onto the counter, he started for the door, halting as Orville Flood and Carla appeared in the entrance and advanced toward him.

"Glad I caught you," Flood said, his sunburned features serious. "Wanted to say everything's all straightened out at the jail."

Shawn made no comment.

"Main thing, however," the man continued,

"was that I was hoping I could get you to reconsider, stay on the job."

"Not a chance," Starbuck said flatly, slinging his saddlebags over a shoulder.

He glanced at the girl. There was neither appeal nor any indication of the displeasure he had seen so often in her eyes, only a sort of regret.

"Can make it worth your while—maybe even get what my brother agreed to pay you doubled."

The corners of Starbuck's mouth tightened. He stirred angrily. "You're wasting your time, Flood! Far as I'm concerned, you're a cheap crook, a slicker out to skin folks who've put their faith and trust in you. I'm no holy-joe, but I'll have no truck with a man like you."

Orville Flood shook his head slowly. "This is politics," he said. "Sometimes things are a bit hard to explain or understand."

"Plain enough for me," Shawn snapped, and pushed on by the man.

"Wait," Carla called after him. "My father owes you something for the time you worked—"

"Forget it," Starbuck answered, without breaking stride—and then came to a complete halt as the girl's scream filled the room.

He spun instinctively, hand coming up fast with his gun. A man had materialized among the chairs in the lobby—a dark, crouched shape with a ragged, torn hat. The rifle he held was leveled at Flood.

Shawn fired, saw the man stagger back, heard the rifle's sharp crack as it went off, sending its bullet into the ceiling of the room. Moving through the floating coils of smoke, he crossed to where the man slumped against a chair, one hand clutching a shoulder. Picking up the rifle, he tossed it into a corner. From just behind him Carla gasped, and then Flood spoke.

"It's Jube Tinker—"

"It's me, all right!" Tinker shouted, eyes burning with hate. "The man you cheated out of his land! Swore I'd get even with you—and I will!"

Starbuck turned away. People were pouring through the hotel's entrance in response to the gunshots, and the pounding of heels in the street indicated that more were on the way. He felt a hand on his arm, paused, looked around. It was Flood, his features taut, desperate.

"Starbuck—you can see how bad I need you! In the name of God, man, help—"

"Not me," Shawn interrupted curtly, and reaching inside his shirt pulled out the hideaway pistol and handed it to the man. "Kind of thing you're mixed up in you'd best start looking out for yourself," he said, and went on.

Breasting the flow, he made his way out onto the hotel's gallery, turned toward the waiting sorrel. Reaching the gelding, he hung his saddlebags behind the cantle, and mounting, cut back into the street. Ogden's voice coming from somewhere in the crowd reached out to him.

"Shawn—where you going?"

"To find my brother," Starbuck answered, and rode on.

Center Point Large Print
600 Brooks Road / PO Box 1
Thorndike, ME 04986-0001 USA

(207) 568-3717

US & Canada:
1 800 929-9108
www.centerpointlargeprint.com